I0817710

THE HIDDEN GIRL

Louise Bassett

WALKER BOOKS
AND SUBSIDIARIES
LONDON • BOSTON • SYDNEY • AUCKLAND

The Hidden Girl
First published in 2025
by Walker Books Australia Pty Ltd
Locked Bag 22, Newtown
NSW 2042 Australia
www.walkerbooks.com.au

Walker Books Australia acknowledges the Traditional Owners of the country on which we work, the Gadigal and Wangal peoples of the Eora Nation, and recognizes their continuing connection to the land, waters and culture. We pay our respect to their Elders past and present.

A catalogue record for this book is available from the National Library of Australia

ISBN: 978 1 761601 64 4

Typeset in 12.5pt Adobe Garamond Pro
Printed and bound in Australia by Griffin Press

EU Authorized Representative: HackettFlynn Ltd,
36 Cloch Choirneal, Balrothery, Co. Dublin, K32 C942, Ireland.
EU@walkerpublishinggroup.com

10 9 8 7 6 5 4 3 2 1

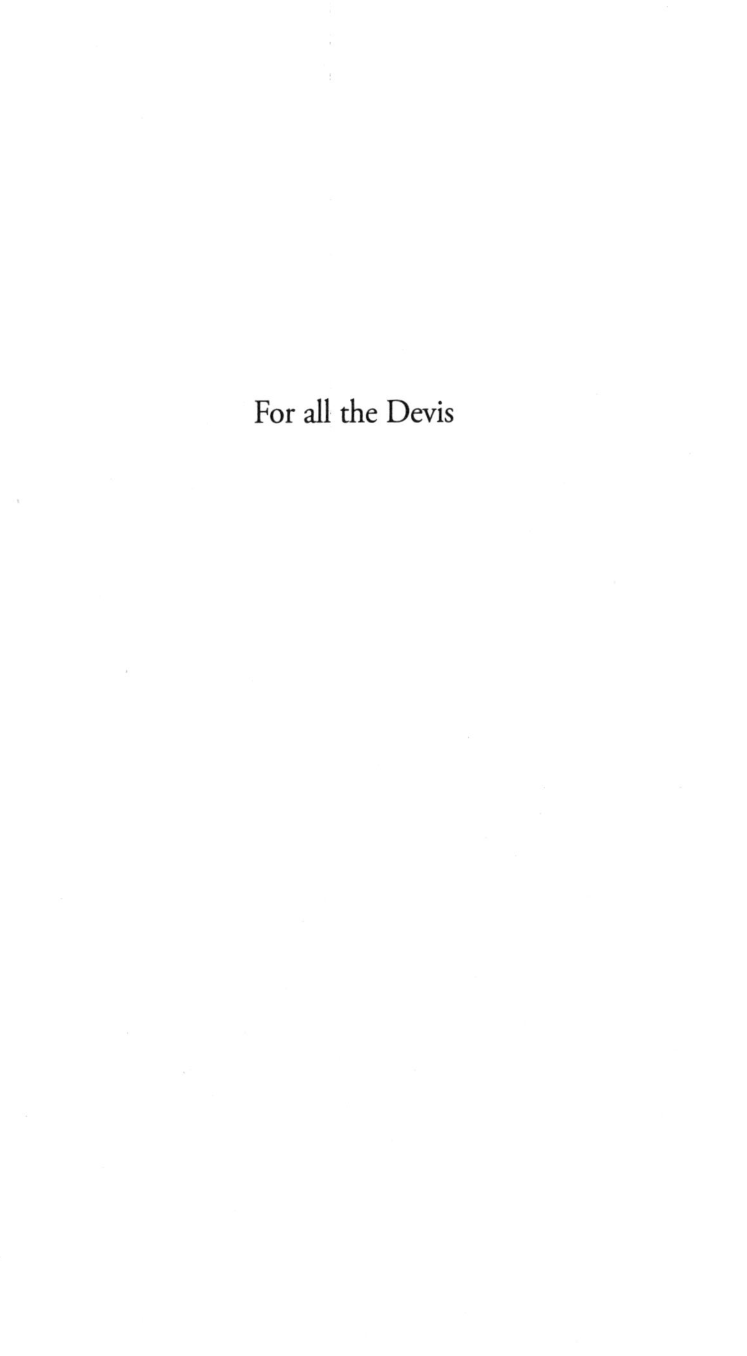

For all the Devis

ONE

Last year when I started at Chisholm it was like I entered a witness protection program and assumed a new identity – Melati Nelson, good girl and total square. I guess I look pretty wholesome, so it hasn't been hard to fool people.

I've made it to Week Ten of Year Eleven, but how long can I keep faking it?

Monday morning, and the school's cast-iron gates loom in front of me. I sigh, shove on my straw hat and step into another world. Everyone's heading for the hall, but I can't face assembly yet and drift in the other direction.

I push open the bright orange door to the locker room. Grace Vincent is sitting on the bench, hunched over. Her shoulders are shaking. I feel as if I've walked in on her in the nude and I want to sneak away, but she must have heard me. I touch her elbow and she flinches.

"What's wrong?" I ask.

She snuffles and tries to catch her breath. In her fist there's a scrunched-up piece of paper that sticks out between her knuckles. For a moment she looks up at me, strands of hair pressed in a damp frame around her forehead, her eyes pink and raw. Then in a rush she shoves past me and pushes through the heavy doors to the restroom.

I stash my backpack in my locker. Grace slams and locks a stall door, so I leave, banging the main door to let her know she's alone. With just minutes until assembly starts, I race through the yard, crushing fallen jacaranda blossoms under my feet.

On my first day at Chis last year Grace spotted me when I strode through the front gates wearing my crispy uniform and heaps of attitude. She showed me around, helped me find my locker and chatted with me all the way to assembly. But we haven't spoken much since then.

I slip through the open door at the back of the hall and find an empty space on the polished floor behind a sea of girls. The headmistress, Mrs. Sturgeon, looks up from the podium. She's classy, with a soft silver bob and kind gray eyes, but she radiates a don't-mess-with-me vibe. That's why we call her the Surgeon.

Rachel sits five rows in front of me. She's trying to be subtle, but she keeps glancing over to the left. The teachers sit along the perimeter of the hall, watching over the cross-legged masses. Her eyes are on Mr. Stokes, the school counselor. Rachel's crush hasn't fizzled out. I don't get it. Not that he's ugly or anything, but he's too old. He must be thirty, at least. Yuck.

The Surgeon is introducing a new junior school teacher, but I tune out and the questions bubble up. Why was Grace so upset? I haven't cried like that since my dog, Austin, died. And that was when I was ten. Maybe I'm hideously shallow.

And what was the paper in Grace's hand? Had someone stuck something awful on her locker?

The Surgeon drones on and on and I sit on my hands to restrain myself from leaving. Last year my urge to break out from the straitjacket of school life scared me. Now I concentrate on the other students to distract myself. Clare Morton has shaved her head to a number 4 – a bold move, and it skirts close to Chis' dress code, but it suits her tiny face. I scan the crowd but I can't find Anne Moens anywhere. She hasn't been around for a week and I can't help worrying about her.

I spot Libby Hartnett at a safe distance. On my first day at Chis I sat with the Year Tens, waiting for assembly. The blonde girl in front of me spun around.

"I'm Libby, Libby Hartnett." Her smile transformed

her face from kind of pretty to striking, and made the new-girl feathers in my stomach settle into a downy nest.

"I'm Melati."

"Melati? Like gelati?"

"Yeah. It's Indonesian."

When she asked me which school I used to go to, the conversation turned.

"Coburg Central?" Libby looked me up and down and raised an eyebrow. "So, you're a charity case then."

My mouth was dry and useless. We weren't poor or anything, but I'd won the Indonesian language scholarship to Chis and saved my parents a ton of money.

Libby gave me a pointed look and turned her back on me. Her work was done: the new girl had been inspected and rejected. I'd only been at Chis half an hour but I could tell from the circle of silence that surrounded us that she was the alpha bitch of Year Ten. My fingers curled into fists, but I'd promised Mum. And she was serious – there would be consequences. I wanted to slap Libby, but I couldn't lose it on my first day. I couldn't lose it at all.

I squared my shoulders and said to Libby's back, "Yeah, the school's paying twenty grand a year for me. Every year. Paying school fees must suck."

The other girls watched for Libby's reaction. She

laughed under her breath and pretended to flick through her hymn book. I used mine as a shield while flipping her off.

On my right, a movement caught my eye – a girl was smirking at me in solidarity. She had dark curls and milky skin that looked as if it had never seen a zit. I grinned back. From that moment Rachel and I were besties.

After assembly Rachel and I make it to Indonesian and grab our usual seats. Even when Libby strolls in, my smile doesn't fade. It's my favorite subject. Thanks to my scholarship, it's the one place at Chis where I feel legit. But I'm no linguistic genius. When I was little we used to live in Indonesia and when we returned to Australia I was a bilingual five year old. Writing and translating are tough, but speaking Indonesian is easier for me.

Ibu Sujati appears and I smile. She looks so cute with her jet black, fortified beehive and Chanel-style suit.

"*Selamat pagi*," she says, the beauty spot above her lip bouncing, her teeth white against fire-engine red lipstick. She rubs her hands together.

"Girls, I hope you're excited about our trip?"

Some of the girls nod, others are still half asleep.

I beam at Ibu Sujati.

"You bet. Can't wait," Rachel says.

Sujati announced the school trip to Indonesia in June last year and I begged Mum and Dad to let me go. I promised to be slave labor for them, whatever it took. They laughed at my shameless groveling and kept me hanging for a couple of torturous days while I did all the vacuuming and dishes and made dinner every night.

"Not long now," Sujati says.

"Nine sleeps." Rachel rests her head against my shoulder and sighs.

Ibu Sujati grabs a stack of papers from her desk. "I've got the updated itinerary here – I managed to squeeze some more excursions in." She strolls between our desks and hands out the flyers.

I scan the itinerary. Jakarta. Jogjakarta. Language school. Sightseeing. Freedom. Temples, steamy sunsets, endless satay sticks. But no volcanoes. Dad trained me from an early age to love them. There are volcanoes close to Jogjakarta, but they're not on the itinerary.

Rachel swings my chair upright and my feet hit the ground. "Excited?"

"Yeah." I smile back at her. "Doesn't feel real though."

"It's going to be so good."

The last few days I've been so grumpy about homework and the grind of school, but now my trip fever has returned and I can't shift the smile from my face.

TWO

The lunch bell rings and girls pour from the classrooms and into the March sunshine. Outside it's like hostile territory with clear but invisible borders. The nerds gather on the steel benches near the library, the athletes drape over the timber play equipment near the new gymnasium or sprawl on the netball courts, the goths and punks hang out in the art studio, darkroom, or car park, and Libby and her bitchy friends claim the sandstone wall nearby.

We're kind of nothings. At least, that's how I feel, even though Rachel, Shanti, and Justine have been here since junior school. In winter we like the timber fort, but while it's still warm we sit under the big fig tree near the netball courts. I call it the "horror movie tree" because it looks like it could swallow you whole, but its gnarly branches and shiny leaves are an umbrella against the sun. Before I sit down I check for possum crap and kick away mangled figs that smell like sweet toffee.

Shanti and I do our usual trade. Mum's lentil burgers for her dad's amazing curry puffs. Rachel watches me squeeze sambal sauce all over them and shakes her head.

I notice a massive graze running the length of Justine's shin. "Waxing accident?"

"Gross, isn't it?" Justine wrinkles her nose, her delicate wire-frame glasses shifting.

"A drinking injury." Shanti smirks.

Shanti stayed with Justine's family at their beach house in Lorne on the weekend. Yup, people have beach houses at Chis. You didn't get that at Coburg Central.

Justine shoots her a warning look.

"She's a lightweight," Shanti says. "One vodka was all it took."

"You can talk. Biggest vomit ever." Justine opens her mouth wide and motions with her hands.

"That's nothing. She fell halfway down a cliff. Could've died if I hadn't dragged her back up." Shanti shakes her head and her lush black ponytail skims her shoulder.

"Can't believe your parents actually let you go." Rachel's cheeks bulge with food.

"I know, right?" Shanti laughs. "They trust Justine, they think she's a nice girl. It's the glasses."

I'm lost remembering my own wasted Year Nine adventures. Vodka and weed were my fuel. Last year I was sober, apart from one relapse last summer when I vomited so hard I burst blood vessels in my eyes. Not a good look.

The girls are watching me, waiting for a response.

"Huh?" I say.

"What about you? Get up to any crazy shit on the weekend?" Shanti says.

"Nope," I say.

"You're always good," Rachel says.

I sink my teeth into the curry puff. Between mouthfuls, I bring up the Indonesian trip. Justine and Shanti make all the right noises, but they don't study Indonesian and they're losing interest.

There's a sudden shout from the netball court. It's Libby standing with her hands on her hips. Grace is sitting in front of her, flinching.

"You slut. Think you can talk shit to me?"

Grace shrinks into Jasmine Saunders, who is sitting beside her.

Libby crouches down and shouts into Grace's face, "You're not going to get away with it, you fucking skank."

We look away and try to eat our lunch but we all watch the netball court through our peripheral vision. We're glad it's not happening to us but ashamed for feeling that way. I cross my legs and dry gumnuts dig into my butt.

"She's found a new Anne Moens," I say, and hope someone will tell me I'm wrong, that it's a one-off.

But they don't.

"Yeah, did you hear?" Rachel says. "Anne couldn't take it anymore. Moved to Ivanhoe Grammar."

Shame taps me on the shoulder. It was last October and I was in the stairwell near the science lab, running down the stairs, late for class. A voice bounced off the concrete walls, one flight down from me.

"Pick. It. Up!" The voice was all sharp edges.

I turned the corner. Pens, books, coins, a hairbrush, even tampons were spewed across the floor. Anne Moens was on her knees, bag beside her, reaching for the brush. She looked up at me, hopeful. Libby brought her foot down on Anne's hand. My mouth opened, but the words lodged in my throat.

Stay out of trouble. Keep your head down.

I slipped past them, raced down the last flight and rocketed out the door. Fresh air hit my face and I hesitated. If I took on Libby I couldn't trust myself to keep up the Good Mel act; I might get into an all-out brawl. I strode away and swallowed hard, but the lump in my throat wouldn't budge. Libby had been working on Anne all year, piling shit on her.

Now Anne has gone. It's not like we were close or

anything, but telling myself that doesn't help.

"What's Libby got against Grace?" I ask.

Rachel leans toward me, an arrowhead frown appearing between her eyebrows. "Libby wanted to go out with Hamish again so she ditched her current boyfriend, but she found out today that Hamish has hooked up with Grace." She chews a corner of her sandwich. "And Grace beat her for the A-grade tennis team. Libby's in the B team for the first time ever."

Last year, Libby used psychological warfare to grind Anne's confidence down. And Libby was sneaky – the teachers never saw her crap. She always pretended to be the perfect student and had a sixth sense for striking when the teachers weren't around. Like now.

"Libby thinks she owns this place," Shanti says.

I gulp when Libby kicks Grace in the back. I will her to fight back, but she just sits there. Jasmine springs to her feet, her hands fluttering. Tiny Jasmine's no match for Libby. I had my share of fights at Coburg, but I've never seen one here. Chis girls don't know how to fight.

But I do.

Get a grip, Mel.

Libby's mates yelp. Are they goading her on? I chew, but the pastry sticks in my throat like cardboard. I bet Libby's behind the paper Grace was holding in the locker room too.

I want to do something, I'm not scared of Libby. But I am scared of myself.

But then Libby shoves Grace's shoulder and I'm on my feet. Rachel tugs at my dress but I shrug her off and stalk toward the netball court. Libby's back is to me. My body prickles with heat.

I suck in a big breath. "Leave her alone!"

Libby turns to look at me, her nostrils flared. Grace stares at the ground. Tension crackles. Everyone is watching.

"What's it to you?" Libby's mouth twists and she pushes Grace.

"Stop it!" I step closer.

"Oh, I'm so scared. It's Gelati the welfare bitch to the rescue."

Things move in slow motion. Libby swings her leg toward Grace and I fly at her, but I can't wrench her away. We struggle, but she sticks to Grace like a limpet. Libby pulls at Grace's shoulders, half-lifts her from the ground, and I grab Libby from behind in a bear hug, but she's too heavy for me to shift. Libby twists to one side, throwing me off and I kick out into space. My foot crashes into the back of her thigh and she wails in exaggerated pain and crumples to the ground.

A voice bellows at me. "Melati Nelson. Stop that right now."

It's Mrs. Pimm.

She grabs my arm and tugs me away. It's bad news when they call me Melati, worse still when it's Pimm. Everyone gawks as my good girl mask shatters into a thousand pieces, leaving a trail from the netball court to the staff room.

THREE

Pimm steers me into a cramped beige room, which is empty apart from a wooden desk and some gray plastic chairs.

"Given your behavior, I'll have to speak to the principal."

"But what—"

Pimm fixes her eyes on me over her green frames.

"But Mrs. Pimm, you don't understand—"

"Sit." She pulls out a chair.

I fling myself into it. "But Libby was—"

"Stay there and don't move while I speak to Mrs. Sturgeon. You need time to think about what you've done." She smooths down her skirt and leaves the room.

What an uptight cow. I stare at the door. Why didn't Pimm haul Libby away too? Libby has gotten away with it. Again.

And what if they expel me? My heart thuds in my chest.

I could bust out of here and run out of Chis, but I'd have to deal with the consequences. I grip the chair and struggle to think, to stay in control, but I find myself at the door. I press my ear to the cool wood and catch faint voices.

"Doesn't sound like her," a male voice says.

". . . red-handed . . . Libby Hartnett," Pimm says.

The male voice laughs. I know that voice.

"You think it's funny?"

"Well, we know what she's like."

It's Mr. Stokes.

"But Libby wasn't kicking anyone," Pimm says.

"Oh, c'mon. What happened before you got there?"

Angry heels clack down the hallway, away from me.

We call her Pimm and Bear It. At first I thought that was harsh, until I had a career counseling session with her and she shredded any ambition I ever had. Some teachers want to help us, some only want a pay check, but the worst ones want to feed on the souls of their teenage prey. Pimm is the original praying mantis.

There's nothing to distract me in here – beige walls, white ceiling, coffee-colored carpet and a cheap plastic black and white clock. My chin drops to my chest. This can't be Year Nine all over again. In our house Year Nine is known as The Year I Stuffed Up. Mum blamed Sarina, said she was too wild and thought that everything would be fine once I'd left Coburg Central, escaped Sarina's clutches and entered the protective confines of the Chisholm School for Girls.

Yeah, right.

Don't get me wrong, blaming Sarina is tempting. But Mum's forgetting something, something she hasn't acknowledged since I was little. I may look innocent, but deep down there's badness in me.

I've got a birthmark on my bum, high on my left cheek. A port-wine stain. It gets darker and darker every year. If you examine it, which is tricky – I have to contort myself to get the mirror at the right angle – it's a definite shape. A pitchfork.

Sarina noticed it the night I tore my jeans when we jumped the fence at East Melbourne Grammar and skinny-dipped in their pool. She teased me that I was the Devil's spawn and a badass. I told her to stop perving at my bum.

In a way I'm proud of my pitchfork. It's like my own private rebellion. A secret tattoo. But on nights when I can't sleep, when the clock tortures me and the dark bends my thoughts into weird shapes, I get to thinking . . .

What if deep down I really am bad?

Forty minutes later the door opens and I stop breathing. It's Dad, with Pimm. She's less threatening with Dad there, even though he looks like he's homeless. He's unshaven, his hair is a mess and he's wearing his shabbiest sweater and the shiny black sweats that make him look like a drug dealer. But he's all I've got right now, so I force a smile. Dad gives me a hang-in-there-kiddo grin. My backpack hangs from his hand.

The pinch returns to Pimm's face. She pushes her glasses higher up the bridge of her nose. "Melati, your father's here to take you home. You've been suspended while we investigate your actions."

I dig my fingernails into my palms.

"We'll be in touch," Pimm says to Dad, as if I'm not there.

We follow her out of the room and they shake hands. Dad thanks her and I hate him for it.

We reach the yard. It's my second walk of shame for today, but this time there are no gawking girls, they're all tucked away in classrooms. Our bronze station wagon is parked out the front under the jacarandas. A bird has already dumped an offering on the windshield and Dad scowls when he notices it.

"Thought you were in Cambodia?" I say.

"Just got home." Dad unlocks the car door, his face

deadpan. "You didn't give me much chance to get over the jetlag." He slides into the car.

I hesitate, then I get in and buckle up. "Got to keep you on your toes. I know how bored you get at home." Being a smart-ass generally works with Dad, but I have to strike the right balance. Too much and he gets annoyed, not enough and he'll think I'm piss weak.

He starts the car and pulls into the traffic. "What happened, Mel?" His hands are white-knuckled around the steering wheel but at least he isn't calling me Melati.

I gather my jumbled thoughts and explain how I ended up kicking Libby.

"You can pick them, kiddo. Isn't that Judge Hartnett's girl?"

I nod.

"Didn't he sponsor the new gym?"

"Yup." I study him – how did he know that? He's never home long enough for school gossip; he must have talked to Mum before picking me up. "Dad, it was all Libby's fault. She never gets in trouble." My voice sounds whiny but I keep going. "Libby does Indonesian and she's going on the trip too. What if they ban me from going?"

Tears build but I swallow them. I'm not going to cry. Dad navigates the back streets of Brunswick. He scratches his chin and I can hear his stubble under his fingernails, his face unreadable. I concentrate on the scene outside. Trees swing their branches in the breeze and we pass an abandoned couch spilling its stuffing. When we pull up outside our house Dad turns to me. I'm convinced he's going to lose his shit.

"You made a big mistake."

"But Dad, she—"

He holds my gaze. "Getting caught, that's all. What you did was right. I'm a pacifist but sometimes force is the only thing a bully understands. I'd rather you get into a bit of trouble for helping someone; too many people stand by and do nothing. I'm proud of you, kiddo." He smiles and his eyes crinkle, the lines cutting deep around his eyes.

Where's the mouthful of blame I was expecting? I grab his arm. "Who are you and what did you do with my dad?" But I can't hold the deadpan like him and I giggle. He laughs along with me before we fall into silence again.

"The truth will turn up. If it doesn't I'll ask them why a sponsor's kid doesn't get the same treatment."

Maybe all will be right in MelatiWorld.

I can't remember the last time I hugged Dad, but now his grotty sweater seems warm and comforting.

After dinner I escape to my room and Hedy rubs up against my shins and purrs. I land on my bed and she dives on to me, her paws digging in, but I shove her aside.

Did I stuff up? The school thinks so, except for Stokes. They'll probably expel me and then . . . I can't even think about it.

My phone beeps. I give in and check it for the first time since this morning. It's loaded with notifications, including one from Jasmine Saunders, Grace's best friend.

Thanks for sticking up for Grace. Hope you're back soon.

I fall back against my pillows and smile.

There are multiple messages and missed calls from Rachel. I open the first:

Wow! My bestie is a secret ninja.

My head swells until I remember my pathetic moves on the court when I couldn't pull Libby away from Grace.

They can't expel you. If they try we'll start a Save Mel campaign. I mean it. We're going on that trip together. It's going to happen. I know it. And Libby deserved it. You were so brave.

They're in my corner, but there's a sour taste in my mouth. It's that word.

Brave.

A lonely trophy of a word. I think of Gandhi, Martin Luther King and Joan of Arc. What did bravery do for them? They're dead, dead, dead. Dead like my school record. They're calling me brave, but deep down they mean stupid. *Thanks for being stupid enough to do what we should have done.*

Outside, Mum pulls up and wheels her cart full of used towels toward the house. I switch off my light and pull the sheet over my head. Hedy sneaks under the covers. There's no way Mum will be as understanding as Dad. She'll think this is The Year I Stuffed Up All Over Again.

But this is different. Defending Grace was the right thing to do. Hedy's ears are like warm velvet under my fingers and I pet them as if it will smooth out all the knots in my chest. A feeling from the netball court floats back to me. In the middle of the fight I felt free, like I was me again. Whatever happens, I have to hold on to that.

FOUR

The moment I glimpse Judge Hartnett over Dad's shoulder I know this is doomed. He dresses like he's ancient, in a navy blazer with gold buttons, and thick gray hair swept back from his puffy face. When I follow Dad into the room the judge places his hand on the back of Libby's chair. For a moment my heart trips; he has this regal vibe that makes you want to beg for mercy. I pull my shoulders back but I'm withering inside.

What a dickhead. No wonder Libby's a power-mad bitch.

For the occasion Dad has changed out of his paint-flecked sweater and into a rumpled shirt. I stand up straighter beside him. He's all blue heeler to Mr. Hartnett's bloated bloodhound.

The Surgeon greets us. Her black and white pinstriped suit is flawless; even creases are too scared to go near her.

"It's been a while." Dad shakes her hand.

"Yes, but sooner than I would've thought," the Surgeon says.

Ouch.

She guides us to a ring of chairs in the middle of the room, set around a low, circular table. Dad approaches Hartnett and they make a big deal out of shaking hands. Libby scowls at me from the other side of the circle. The bitchy curl of her lip makes me want to punch her.

I need to get a grip. Fast.

Mr. Stokes lopes into the room, looking like he's dragged himself from the beach with his tousled sandy hair, sunglass marks on his nose and Birkenstocks on his feet. He shakes hands with Dad and Hartnett.

Stokes is running this crazy gig. The day after I was suspended Dad and I met with Stokes and one of the assistant principals. They asked me a thousand questions about what happened and were also interviewing Libby and Grace and other witnesses. Now, we're having this "restorative circle meeting to try and put things right." It sounded OK when Stokes first said it, but when I look at Libby and her dad I want to run from the room.

The Surgeon looks around the circle. "Thanks to all of you for putting the time aside to come here and work things out."

Libby watches me from under her fringe. Hartnett kicks his feet out in front of him and crosses his ankles.

The side of the Surgeon's mouth twitches. "Water, anyone?"

Hartnett passes us two of the plastic cups on the table and I mutter a thank you. I wonder if they chose plastic on purpose, like at an underage gig, so we can't hurl missiles at each other.

"Chisholm uses circle meetings to help repair relationships after something has gone wrong," the Surgeon says.

Hartnett pulls at the knot of his tie, loosening it a little.

"We find them more useful than traditional methods, as do many other schools, especially if participants are willing to keep an open mind." She nods to Stokes.

He cups his hands together between his knees. "Thanks Evelyn. Circle meetings aren't new, they're an ancient way of repairing relationships after conflict. Our Maori neighbors have used them for centuries."

"Philippine hill tribes too," Dad says.

Stokes nods. "They're important in a school environment where we all need to try and get along." He looks around the circle like we're gathered around a campfire to tell ghost stories. I'm waiting for him to break out the Native American headdress, but he launches into the rules: he'll lead and we'll all get to speak, then we'll work out a plan to improve things.

We're going around in circles all right. Why can't they tell me my punishment and put me out of my misery? This is torture. Libby and I will never get along.

"Sounds like poppycock to me," Hartnett says.

The Adam's apple bobs in Stokes' throat. "I'm glad you said that because I was skeptical when I first heard about circle meetings, but I've seen them work many times. Why not give it a try?"

Hartnett uncrosses his ankles and sits upright but says nothing.

"Libby, can you tell us what happened?" Stokes says.

"Well, I was talking to Grace and Jasmine. Just talking. Then out of nowhere, Melati attacked me," Libby says in her sweetest, girliest voice.

What the fuck? "That is not what happened." My voice rises.

"Melati, you'll get your turn in a moment." Stokes holds up his hand. "Go on, Libby. When you say 'attacked,' what actually happened?"

"She did this weird bear hug thing," Libby motions with her arms, "and tried to drag me away. Then she kicked me in the back of my leg."

I grip the sides of my chair as Libby spins her fake version.

Dad rests his hand on my arm for a moment. I'm not sure if it's to comfort me or to stop me from jumping up and slapping Libby.

Then finally Stokes turns to me. "Melati, why don't you tell us your version of events?"

Uh oh.

It's like he's asked me to bungee jump, but what the hell. I clear my throat and describe how Libby picked on Grace. Stokes asks me to be more specific, so I get up and imitate Libby's actions. The Hartnetts' eyes burn me, but Stokes manages to keep them quiet, holding up both his hands, like a conductor silencing an orchestra, until he draws the whole story from me.

"Anything else you want to add?" Stokes says.

I take a deep breath. "Yeah, that Libby is totally lying. Ask my friends or Grace and they'll tell you."

"You're going to let her get away with that?" Hartnett says. "It's hardly fair that the culprit—"

Stokes wields the hands of silence again. "Judge, I have the utmost respect for what you do in court but this is a different process and I would ask you to go with that." He scratches the side of his nose and light glints on his chunky silver wedding band. "And it would help if we could avoid using blaming words."

A vein is pulsing in Hartnett's temple.

"Melati, your friends backed up what you said. But Libby's friends backed up her account," Stokes says. "Unfortunately, Grace didn't want to participate today but her version of events matches Libby's."

All the air is sucked out of me as Stokes' words crash around in my head. Grace lied too.

"Well, there you have it," Hartnett says.

I shake my head. "Grace must have been too scared to tell the truth because she knows what Libby's like."

Stokes meets my eyes. "Go on."

Hartnett reaches for Libby's hand. He squeezes it, keeping his hand low. Libby catches me watching and tugs her hand away.

I tell them about Grace crying in the locker room. "She wouldn't tell me what was wrong but it was obvious. Everyone knows Libby's bullied other people before, like Anne Moens. Grace didn't want to be a target—"

"This is rubbish!" Hartnett rises from his chair. He points a finger at Stokes. "And no more of you silencing me. I won't have Libby defamed by this little . . . this trash! She's lying and I won't sit here any longer and take it. To think I rearranged court for this."

Libby stiffens in her chair.

"Now, Mr. Hartnett." The Surgeon extends a hand toward him.

He blocks her hand. "I'm not one of your students. When I think of all the money I pay this school."

Libby's been silent for the longest time.

Hartnett jabs a finger in my direction. "I'd be better off reporting her to the police."

I flinch.

Hartnett grabs Libby's hand and tugs her out to the hallway. The Surgeon charges after them. A pale-faced Stokes apologizes and follows them.

"This is going well." Dad rubs his hands together.

"Are you crazy?" I say. "My life's going to shit and you think it's funny." I slump against my chair.

"Don't you see, kiddo?" He glances at the door and lowers his voice. "They're stuck. If they wanted to expel you, they would've done it already. But I suspect they know Libby's no angel. There would have been complaints in the past."

"Grace didn't help."

"She didn't, but they're trying to find a way around it, keep faith with the rest of the girls and not have Hartnett tear up his check book into the bargain. The judge isn't making it easy. And Stokes is in over his head. He must have hoped the truth would come out. He's probably done one training course and thought he was ready for this." Dad inches closer. "I think Hartnett would've taken a slug at you if the rest of us hadn't been here. Like father like daughter, I guess."

I don't mention that I wanted to punch Libby's lights out when I entered the room. I rub my temples. Dad's words settle and it's like switching from black and white to color. Maybe he's right. "But he called me trash."

"He was emotional."

"What if he goes to the police, like he said?" My stomach, knotted already, branches out into macramé.

"Think about it, the police would do an investigation, dig up all sorts of stuff, like that other girl . . ."

"Anne."

"He wouldn't want that. Imagine if the press got hold of it."

I hope he's as smart as he sounds. "What was that about Philippine hill tribes?"

He rubs his hand over his mouth. "Oh, I made that up. Just trying to help Mr. Stokes."

The Surgeon catches up with the Hartnetts and convinces them to return – but not to the same room as us. Over the next couple of hours poor Stokes pings back and forth between the two rooms, negotiating between us. The Surgeon stays with the Hartnetts, I guess to stop them from bolting again. With each round of demands

Stokes wilts further. Dad says the whole process is more draining than an international climate change summit.

The Hartnetts demand that I write an apology to Libby and I agree, on condition that Libby writes one to Grace. They drop the apology.

The clock is marching toward 6.30 pm, when Stokes enters the room and hands me the draft agreement. He collapses into a chair. "I feel like a Jack-in-a-box, one that someone's forgotten to wind up." He rubs his eyes.

The paper shakes in my hand. "*Behavioral Contract*? Seriously? Makes me feel like I'm in juvie." Shades of Year Nine. I groan and face plant on the table.

"It's pretty standard," Stokes says.

Standard? What kind of crazy universe does he live in?

"Dad, what do you think?"

He scans the contract and I watch him, my shoulders tight. He passes it back to me. "It's got to be up to you, Mel. You're the one who has to live with it."

All the lectures he's given me and now he's leaving this one to me?

Great. Just great.

They wait for my answer. I know they're both dying to go. After three hours I'd agree to almost anything to get out of the room – maybe that was Stokes' devious plan all along. Libby's signature is at the bottom. All it would take is a few swoops of the pen to join her. I force myself to concentrate on the words.

BEHAVIORAL CONTRACT

Elizabeth Hartnett and Melati Nelson agree to the following:

(a) Melati to attend anger management counseling for the remainder of the school year. In return the Hartnetts agree not to contact the police.

(b) Melati and Elizabeth will have no contact with each other, except what is unavoidable at school and on the Indonesian trip. They will not badmouth or speak publicly about each other.

(c) They will report any issues to a teacher but will not confront each other directly. There shall be no further violence.

(d) If any condition is broken the student concerned will be banned from the Indonesian trip and dealt with in accordance with Chisholm's Suspension and Expulsion Policy.

When I read section (a) my jaw hurts. Libby attacks Grace and I'm the one getting counseling? It's crap, but at least they're not going to expel me. If I don't sign, the Hartnetts' promise not to contact the cops will disappear. Despite what Dad said, can I take that chance?

And if I don't sign things could drag on and I could miss out on the Indonesian trip. My heart twists like someone is wringing it out. Indonesian is the one solid thing I've had since Year Nine. Can I risk that?

FIVE

With my suspension over, I watch girls stream through the schoolyard to morning classes. I tilt my hat to cast a shadow over my face and make a dash for my appointment with Stokes. I don't want to deal with Libby's smug face, but apart from a few curious looks, I avoid nearly everyone on my run to his office.

Reggae music sneaks under the gap between his office door and the dated marmalade-colored carpet in the hallway. I knock and Stokes snuffs the music.

"Come in," he says.

I open the door. A bookshelf – packed full of books, records, and trinkets – divides the room, like he's giving you space to take a deep breath before you sit down and tell him everything. Stokes swivels around in his chair to face me.

"Reporting in for anger management." I salute him.

He laughs and waves me to a wicker armchair opposite his desk.

"Glad it's not a couch," I say.

"Yeah, most students would find that a bit intimidating. I'm no Freud."

The only thing I know about Dr. Freud is that penis envy stuff, which I keep to myself. I drop my backpack and sit down. He places a manila folder on the coffee table between us.

"Is that my psycho profile?"

"You've got this all worked out, haven't you?" He opens the file and hands me two pieces of paper. "That's all that's in there."

The first is the dreaded Behavioral Contract. The second is a copy of an email to my parents from the scholarship committee, warning that I've got one strike against me. Two more and I'll be out.

"What would you like to talk about?" He squeezes the bridge of his nose.

"Don't you tell me?" I cross my arms.

"Look, from what I've seen, I don't think you've got an anger problem."

"Can you write that down and sign it, for my mum?"

Stokes laughs. "You're only here because it's what we negotiated with the Hartnetts. Let's try and make it useful for you. OK, Melati?"

His honesty knocks me out. Ever since Pimm hauled

me away from the netball court I've stepped into a world of half-truths and weirdness where no one says what they mean.

"Call me Mel."

He rests his hands on his knees. "What made you act on the netball court?"

"I don't know." I twist my peace ring around my finger.

"C'mon, Mel."

"What's the point? Everyone thinks I'm a liar who attacked Libby for no reason."

"The way I see it there's what really happened and then there's what you can prove. So tell me."

Is he saying he believes me? Something loosens in my chest.

He nods, urging me on.

"It was when Libby kicked Grace."

"Was there anything else you could've done to stop her without getting physical?"

It's hard to think past the tunnel vision I had in the schoolyard. "Find a teacher? But by the time I'd found one it would have been too late."

"It might be good to explore other ways you could defend someone. Mrs. Sturgeon's in the same boat as me, we can't condone violence, but there's self-defense and the need to defend others. We don't want to discourage people from acting nobly."

I blink at him. "You think I was *noble*?"

Stokes smiles and for a moment – a totally awkward moment – I understand Rachel's crush. His eyes scrunch up when he smiles and he has a cheeky, boyish energy about him.

Woah, girl, don't go there.

"It's rare that people put themselves on the line, but when they do they step into a gray zone. There aren't easy answers for teachers, or for students."

Stokes talks about how noble I was and I sit there like a massive hypocrite. Maybe it was Libby's taunt that pushed me over the edge, not the kick. *Welfare bitch.* The words still sting.

"What's wrong?"

"It's just –" How much can I say? Will they use it against me?

"Whatever is said in here is confidential." Stokes clutches his hands like he's praying for me to trust him.

"What makes me mad is I'm here, like I'm the bad guy, and what's Libby doing? Nothing. She kicked a girl. Kicked her. In front of us. All those anti-bullying sessions they made us sit through last year telling us not to be a bystander. Well, I wasn't and what do I get for it? A big fat strike against my record. She gets nothing. It's a huge pile of bull."

He brushes his hair back from his face. "Look, I can understand how you feel, but we're not ignoring what's going on. You don't know everything. I mean—" He rubs his hand over his mouth and forces a smile. "Are you concerned about being on the trip with Libby?"

"What were you—"

"How are you going to deal with it if she annoys you on the trip?"

"I don't know. Talk to Rache, or the teachers if it gets bad, I guess."

There's a framed photo on his desk of a group of climbers, all guys except for one woman with honey-blonde hair and green eyes who stands closest to Stokes. She grins into the camera, an intimidating mountain peak behind her. Her expression is warm and tender.

"Is that your wife?"

His glance flickers toward his desk then locks on me. "What about a diary? That might help."

"No way. I don't do diaries."

"I keep one. Helps me keep things in perspective."

"They're so embarrassing." When my brother Samuel found the diary I kept in Year Nine he threatened to tell Mum and Dad everything, but never did. Still, I wasn't going there again.

"Don't read what you write, just get it down. Do it

in invisible ink if you like. Think of it as a travel journal with a bit of ranting space." He tilts his head and the sunlight catches the blond tones in his hair. "After all, Rache might get sick of hearing about it."

I laugh but shake my head. We chat about protecting myself online but I tune out. I nod at the right moments but it's like watching Netflix with the volume muted. I can't hear him through all my thoughts.

There's a knock at the door. Insistent. Stokes crosses the room in a couple of strides and speaks to someone in hushed, urgent tones. He swings around, his hand still clutching the doorknob.

"Sorry, Mel, I've got to duck out. Stay put, I should only be a minute."

He bolts from the room and the door swings shut behind him.

I'm alone. Alone in his office. Is he crazy? Stokes of all people should know where temptation can lead girls like me. For a second, I sit there, but then I'm on my feet, in full snoop mode. Rachel would kill for an opportunity like this.

There are photos on the wall of Stokes surfing, rock climbing and traveling, like he's trying to remind himself of when his life was exciting. I'm fiddling with a jade Buddha on his desk when I freeze. What if this is a test?

I'm in enough trouble already. I tiptoe to the door, turn the handle and peek through the slimmest of cracks, but the hallway is an empty stretch of marmalade-colored carpet and closed office doors. I swing around and scan the room for hidden cameras, then shrug off my paranoia.

Seriously, pull yourself together.

His bookshelf is a yawn. *Cognitive Behavior Therapy Made Easy*, *Understanding Millennials*. I check out his vinyl collection: reggae, soul and something called ska.

I wander back to the cane chair and flop in it. That's when I notice the key in the cabinet under his desk. His files must be in there. I remember how he started to say something about Libby – has he counseled her? Then she'd have a file. *There's what really happened and then there's what you can prove.* His words tease me. Maybe there's something on Libby's file that could help me clear my name, something she told him in confidence. I yank the drawer open. It's packed with hanging files and it's difficult to read the labels because the files are jammed together. "Sabine Fischer," "Romy Harrison." His files are out of order and the labels are missing on some of them; Libby's file could be anywhere. With a glance at the door, I keep digging and near the back there's a file for "Grace Vincent." My fingers pause.

At the very back of the cabinet there's a file labeled "L H" in faint pencil. Libby's file? A voice curls in my ear, telling me to take it. With a last glance at the door, I pull the file from the drawer. The contents are heavy.

A floorboard squeaks outside the door and I stuff the file in my backpack, shove the drawer shut and dive back into my seat. Stokes enters and I act casual, even though my heart is busting through my ribs.

He's rubbing his forehead and his face is pale. "Sorry, Mel. I've got to deal with something. Anyway, we've almost used up our time. Same bat time, same bat channel next week?"

"Sure." What's with the bat references? I'll have to ask Mum. Holding my backpack close to my body, I slink past him.

With ten minutes until English, I head to the seniors' restroom, the one place at Chisholm where I can be alone.

It's all Libby's fault. If she weren't such a total bitch I wouldn't be sitting on the lid of a toilet, breathing through my mouth to block out the rank cocktail of urine and disinfectant. I never would have found the file. I never would have been in the school counselor's office. I never would have played the hero and been suspended.

If Libby were different I'd be in class now, minding my own business, like I did all through Year Ten. But last year is another planet now.

Someone opens the main door to the restroom. I hold my breath and hope they won't notice me. They lock a stall a few doors down from mine. My backpack burns on my lap and I will myself to wait. I read the stall door graffiti:

LAUREN'S A BITCH

YOUR THE BITCH

The bad grammar bugs me.

CHIS IS A HELLHOLE

I trace the angry swoops of the black marker and smile. Chis has a zero-tolerance policy on graffiti, but then Chis has a zero-tolerance policy on everything. The caretaker paints over the permanent marker and the occasional spray-painted graffiti as soon as it appears, like a gardener attacking weeds. But like weeds, graffiti finds a way to survive.

A trumpet noise fills the restroom. I muffle my laughter. Water thunders into the toilet bowl and I seize my chance, yank the zip open on my backpack and pull out the blue suspension file. I press it between my hands, feeling the bulk inside it, until the main door swings and I'm alone again. Me and the humming cisterns.

I play with the plastic label sticking up from the file.

It's personal, private.

But Libby lied through her teeth. And now they think I'm the liar.

They'll expel you if they catch you.

It's just one little act of badness and look where being good has got me.

I open the file and blink. Inside there are a few pages – print outs from an online translation site – and a beautiful oxblood leather book covered in small stamps. Like a handmade diary. Libby's diary? The leather looks well-loved. I run my finger over the stamped patterns of flowers, reeds, and villagers. I release the tab on the diary and the creamy pages spring open to the first entry. The handwriting slopes forward. But this can't be right. I flick through the pages – they're all the same. I stare at the handwriting, blink at it even, but it stares back at me, unchanged.

It's written in Indonesian.

What the hell?

SIX

I yell out, before I remember that I shouldn't have. When Samuel left for his gap year, Mum transformed his bedroom and sometimes treats clients there. I'm not supposed to yell. *It's unprofessional and ruins the mood for the clients. Breaks the serenity.*

Sorry serenity.

But I'm home alone. Hedy stops licking herself and follows me to the kitchen. I stop dead in front of the fridge. The brochure for the Rokesby School is back, under a smiley face magnet on the freezer door. It first appeared in Year Nine and disappeared after I started at Chis.

The photo creeps me out. Lush farmland, a two-storey mansion and freshly scrubbed teenagers standing with their shoulders back and forced smiles, adults by their sides. "Established in 1999, the Rokesby School is a caring, alternative school. Rokesby helps students get back on track, with wilderness challenges and one-on-one mentoring . . ."

"Wilderness challenges" is a dead giveaway. This is Brat Camp. Even more tragic, it's in a grim country town in New South Wales where my nan lives. Mum and Dad had talked about boarding school if Chis didn't work out, but I thought it was a scare tactic and didn't think they'd want to waste their money. But they could always stash me at Nan's.

Lucky me.

With a marker I draw Hitler moustaches on the adults and straitjackets on the kids. I turn the yellow smiley face magnet upside down and step back to admire my work.

There's a massive collage of photos on the fridge and my eyes fall on a photo of Dad holding the toddler version of me in his arms in front of Mount Bromo, a white horse and rider beside us. Vapors hang in the air and it looks like Dad's about to sacrifice me to the volcano gods by throwing me into the hungry crater.

Below the Bromo shot, there's an old photo of Oma, my gran, when she was my age, just before her family fled Indonesia for Australia. She's in her school uniform, with her cheeky smile and her hair backcombed into a ponytail. There's a dimple in her right cheek – just like mine. Oma taught me my first words of Indonesian and stayed with us for a few months when we lived in Indonesia. Back then we were really close, and looking at her photo now makes me smile. I peel it from the fridge and place it on the kitchen counter.

I grab the diary from my backpack. For the second time today I stare at the bouncy handwriting and the Indonesian words of the first entries. Ink sketches of faces flicker between the pages, like images from a kid's flip book. There's a dreamy Asian guy with floppy hair and soft eyes, a striking woman with curls and wide cheekbones, and a young Asian woman with long lush hair. Later there's a man's handsome face, all sharp cheekbones and hard lines. His eyes challenge me and I snap the diary shut, drop it on the counter and shove it away.

I open my math book. Equations blur on the page. I chew my pen and wrestle with the problems, but questions crowd me. There's no way Libby could have written the diary. Her Indonesian is good, but not that good. And why does Stokes have it? Who are the people in the drawings?

The print outs from the file don't help – it looks like someone plugged some text into a translator but the results are a mess. Words like "goddess," "fifteen," and "school" are strung together in a way that doesn't make sense.

There are question marks in the margins, lines drawn between words and phrases, and a big fat question mark at the bottom of the page. Is it Libby's handwriting? Or Stokes'?

If Stokes notices the file is missing and works out that I took it, they'll probably expel me. I have to return it. I'll slip it back into his filing cabinet first chance I get.

I squeeze my eyes shut for a moment to silence my thoughts and return to my homework. *If y=3x, state the x and y intercept of this linear relation ...*

There could be something in there that helps me prove Libby's a liar. The diary is a code I haven't cracked. How can I resist when I have the key?

1 October

Devi means "goddess," but try telling my family that. When I get home it's like slamming into a wall. Rusli, Inan, and Dian tug my arms, climb on me, tangle their fingers in my hair. *Read me a book, give me a hug, I'm hungry, make her stop.*

They don't care how I feel, as long as they get what they need.

Then Mum and Dad start: *Devi, can you cook dinner? Devi, can you chop some wood?*

Devi, can you, can you, can you?

It's so bad I hate hearing my name.

Goddess. What kind of joke is that?

No wonder Irianto left, it's no fun being the eldest. I wish I didn't look older. Mum and Dad forget I'm only fifteen and they expect more from me. Since Dad's accident they're even worse and there's no time for homework. They don't understand why anyone would want to read or draw or sing. They want a slave.

At school it's different – I'm special there. Everyone wants to be my friend. Ibu Yuliana is an angel. She gives me poetry to inspire my songwriting, art books to fire my imagination and this diary to lift me up. I wouldn't survive without her.

Devi, *Devi* – that's a girl's name. I stand up from the table and stretch my arms and neck. It doesn't make any sense. This isn't Libby's diary. Or even her file. Why would Stokes have an Indonesian schoolgirl's diary in his filing cabinet? I stare at Oma's photo, but she's no help.

Later

I told Mum and Dad I wanted to be a *dangdut* singer and they laughed at me. *They laughed!* I couldn't believe it. They said I'm *selling myself too high*, but I don't want to live like them. I don't want to end up with a mangled leg like Dad's and hands as tough as bamboo. They have no ambition.

I should never have told them. Of course they wouldn't understand.

But they won't kill my dream.

I snuck out of the house, wove around houses and ran through the field so no one could follow me and climbed up my tree. Up here I always feel better.

When I was little I used to dress up and perform. Mum and Dad loved it, but that all changed. I don't know why. Now they stop me if I show off, like they're embarrassed.

They can't really be my parents.

I wish I lived with Ibu Yuliana. We'd talk about art and poetry all day and she'd encourage my singing and drawing. She wouldn't stomp all over my dreams.

I was born into the wrong family.

A few pages on there's an E near the top of the page. On the next page a P. Underlined letters are scattered throughout the diary. Randomly. A final H in Devi's last entry two weeks ago. I write them down.

EPHLEMREETHGGINOOTLIKLEMNIREEH

Weird.

I stare at the letters, willing them to rearrange themselves into something that makes sense. There must be a bunch of words in there, but how do I break up the letters? It must be a secret code, like we used when we were kids. Samuel and I became obsessed with them one summer and used up all the lemons we could find to make invisible ink.

A car pulls up outside. It sounds like Dad's. I slide Oma's photo inside the diary, stash it in my backpack and return to my math book. The house is dark apart from the pool of light on the kitchen table.

I've stretched every brain cell to understand Devi's words, but some of them I don't get, like *dangdut*. Translating is tough. It's like I've been cutting through thick jungle with a pocket knife. But now I'm glimpsing this girl's life through the small parting I've made in the undergrowth.

But Mr. Stokes, what the hell?

What are you doing with her diary?

The question turns on me: Why have I got her diary? I squirm inside and promise to return it as soon as I can.

SEVEN

With my bottom-heavy backpack I look like a weird insect searching for a safe place to lay larvae. I burn past hyper kids, lovers sharing last kisses, and passengers tugging overstuffed bags through Melbourne's airport. My backpack slams against my butt. I need to pee and I'm cursing Dad for taking so long to leave the house. Finally I spot the Chis group in Departures and stagger over to them.

Ibu Sujati smiles, checks me off her list and scans the crowd for the remaining girls in our group. Ms. Krantz, the sports teacher and the other chaperone for the trip, takes over the clipboard. Kransky looks like she's dressed for one of her iron woman training sessions, with an aqua T-shirt, black running tights, and fluoro pink sneakers.

Chis girls talk non-stop – squeal, jump around, and crash into each other like two year olds after a red cordial transfusion. Rachel dashes over to me, her cheeks glossy, and spins me around. I start to topple, but she props me up and I wriggle free of my backpack.

"Can you believe it?" she says. "We're really going!"

I grin. Since the fight with Libby I've been on my best behavior, worried that I'd stuff up, or that Libby would trip me up. But I've survived.

Grace has been weird though. When I tried to approach her she gave me the big swerve. You'd think I'd kicked her in the back. Stokes told me not to take it personally – he thinks I remind her of that time and her feelings of humiliation. How twisted is that?

Libby is on the edge of our group. The woman beside her clutches Libby's forearm. She's gorgeous, with wavy dark hair and deep blue eyes. Judge Hartnett isn't in sight.

"That's her aunt. They're real close," Rachel says. "Her mum's not around so her aunt helps out."

"What do you mean her mum's not around?"

Rachel's mum, Mrs. Olliver-Beckwith-Brown, or Mrs. OBB for short, launches herself at us. She's scrawny with wild red highlights in her black hair and high eyebrows that make her look permanently surprised.

"Now, darling." She drapes an arm around Rachel's shoulders. "You've got those poo-stopper tablets, haven't you?"

"Seriously, Mum." Rachel rolls her eyes.

"You'll be thanking me when you're huddled over a squat toilet not knowing which end to put over the bowl. I remember one time with your father in China—"

"Get her away from me." Rachel ducks behind me and I quiver with laughter.

My parents stride up, breathless after their run from the car park. I'd left them there to fight it out – Mum was furious with Dad for taking his "sweet old time" to leave the house, then driving like a maniac on the freeway. Dad couldn't understand what the fuss was about. He's such a frequent flyer he disregards basic laws of physics like speed, distance and airport check-in times. But now their smiles reach their eyes when they greet everyone.

"Girls, you'll look after each other, won't you?" Dad says.

I nod. "Yeah, Dad."

Dad rubs the side of his nose, then turns away to read the updates on the Departures board. A lazy smile spreads across his face. Airports are Dad's happy place.

Mum lays both hands on my shoulders and it's my turn to squirm. "You won't go anywhere near drugs, will you?"

Years ago a young Australian woman was busted with weed in her boogie board bag and sentenced to twenty years in a Balinese jail. Mum has never recovered.

"Bugger." I slap my palm against my forehead. "Forgot to bring my boogie board."

Rachel giggles behind me.

"Mel, I'm serious. Different rules apply there and some people are desperate. Be careful." Mum frowns and I notice the little lines radiating from her eyes and across her forehead. She's got to stop stressing so much, I'm not *that* stupid.

"Tampons? You packed them, didn't you? Some Muslim countries are funny about them," Mrs. OBB says.

"Just kill me now," Rachel says.

Dad snaps back to parental attention. "You packed your EpiPen?"

"Yes, Dad." One near-death-from-seafood experience is enough for one lifetime, thank you very much.

Ibu Sujati and Kransky return from the group check-in counter, wave our boarding passes in the air, and start to round us up. A domino wave of farewell hugs and kisses sweeps through our group. Dad squeezes me, then I hug Mum and whisper that she doesn't have to worry, I won't be an idiot. Her eyes well up and she turns away, her head low. Our group starts to walk away and there's a lump in my throat now – this trip will be the longest I've ever been away from my parents. Two whole weeks. I wave goodbye until the departure gates swallow us.

Through the plastic porthole the sunset is a dusky pink. Baggage handlers in high-vis uniforms throw our luggage on to a conveyor belt. My skin's tingling, I can't stop smiling and we haven't even taken off.

A flight attendant in a blue Garuda uniform offers us lollies from a basket. I pick one and roll it over in my mouth.

"Not bad. Reminds me of something." I read the wrapper. "Durian flavored."

Rachel spits hers into an airsickness bag. "More like ear wax."

The safety demo begins and I try to forget every episode of *Air Crash Investigation* I've ever watched. When I look behind me for the nearest exit, there's Libby stretching out her legs in the emergency exit aisle about eight rows back.

Great, she'll trip me over if we have to evacuate.

Ever since the circle meeting disaster there's been an invisible barrier separating us. She's even left Grace alone. Dad reckons Judge Hartnett would've been breathing down Libby's neck and, like me, she didn't want to risk being banned from the trip.

Within minutes we're rolling, a steel bullet speeding down the runway. I hold my breath as we take off. Houses, swimming pools, and roads shrink as we climb into the clouds.

"Goodbye Melbourne, *selamat malam* Indonesia," Rachel says.

My ears pop, and after a few minutes the flight attendants serve drinks and dim the cabin lights. Rachel curls up against the window and falls asleep. Great company. I'm dead jealous of her narcolepsy because I've got no chance of sleeping, so I fish around in my bag for entertainment. My tablet's pre-loaded with illegal downloads and I stuff it into the pocket of the seat in front of me.

When I find the diary my chest rises. If Stokes had left me alone in our last session I would have returned it, but he didn't. For the last week I've been translating the most interesting chunks of the diary, mainly when I can't sleep. It's hard going, and sometimes I skip bits, but it's improving my Indonesian. Oma would be proud. I'm getting nowhere with the coded message though. It must be an anagram but I can't crack it; there are too many letters. I've held a mirror up to it and typed it into an online Indonesian anagram solver, but nothing works. It's so frustrating.

Devi's life is depressing as hell. All she does is go to school or slave away for her parents – they never give her a break. She should build a permanent tree house in that tree of hers.

13 October

Ibu Yuliana is MY HERO! Today she gave me a pamphlet for the Bandung Performing Arts College. I'd never heard of it. It's a high school where you study normal subjects, like math, along with singing, dance, and drama. You can chase your dream while you finish school.

I'm so excited. Next year I'll audition, and if my singing's good enough I might win a full scholarship. I'll be able to train with real singers. But my grades have to be good. I'm going to study my heart out – I'd be crazy not to. This is a sign. It's everything I've been waiting for.

18 October

Something amazing happened tonight. I ran to my tree to start the new book of poetry Ibu Yuliana gave me, but halfway up I heard someone at the top. I froze and clung to the trunk. My heart sank, but then this invader hung down from a high branch and smiled at me.

His name's Budi and he's from Manado, which explains his dark skin. He just moved here with his mum and goes to the Christian college in the city. We sat on the two strongest branches and I tried to read some poems, but I couldn't concentrate. He kept chipping at this piece of wood, slicing off chunks with his knife.

I gave up and drew a little – first the sunset and then, when he wasn't looking, I drew him.

19 October

Budi is the sweetest. He's nothing like the boys at school. Tonight he gave me a present, a tiny dove he'd carved. I couldn't stop smiling. The detail is amazing, you can see feathers etched into the wood. It's beautiful. I've hidden it under my bed so the little ones won't steal it. Just knowing it's there makes me smile. He made it for me.

Something bumps the back of my chair. My ribs crash into my tray and my can of Coke tips over. Bubbling brown liquid pours over my legs and the pages of the diary.

"Oh, Mel, I'm so sorry! Look at your pants." Libby is towering over me, hanging on to the top of my chair. She swings herself back into the aisle and stands up. Marnie, one of her minions, is behind her.

Some of the Coke drains on to the floor, the rest soaks through my pants, a brown stain creeping from my crotch to my knees. I jump from my seat and the diary crashes to the floor. I grab some tissues and dab at the stain but it's useless. My hands are shaking and when I catch Libby smirking at Marnie I could punch her.

Why the hell not? It's not like they can throw me off the trip now. But thoughts of Mum's worried face, my scholarship, and brat camp flash before me at warp speed. I dab harder.

"Can I do anything to help?" Libby's eyes shine.

I glare at her.

"It was an accident. You know, the turbulence." She crosses her arms and sticks out her chin.

I count to ten and try to control my breathing like Stokes trained me to do. But when I reach five the tissues disintegrate and my jaw stiffens. We lock eyes.

Don't lose it. Don't lose it. Don't lose it.

"What's going on?" Rachel rouses and stands up next to me.

"Nothing," Libby says. "Anger management must be working." She loops a piece of hair behind her ear. "I wonder, what *do* they get up to in their sessions?"

That's it, I'm going to beat her up.

Rachel moves closer and grips my fist. "Think you're funny, don't you?" She points her finger down the aisle. "Piss off."

Libby puts one hand on her hip and doesn't budge.

"Go on. Piss off," Rachel says again.

Turbulence rocks the plane and Libby crashes into the chair across the aisle from me.

The man sitting there twists around and glares at her. "Watch what you're doing, you could've damaged my laptop."

The seat belt sign flashes back on.

Libby grabs Marnie's arm and they slink back down the aisle.

"I hate that bitch," Rachel says.

"I almost lost it."

"Coke pants will do that to you."

I pluck my pants from my legs and sigh – five more hours with a soggy crotch. But as soon as the seat belt sign goes off Rachel squeezes past me. She rummages in the overhead locker and passes me a pair of yoga pants. "Mum made me pack them. She's paranoid about lost luggage. And tampons." She rolls her eyes.

"You're my hero." I hug her and dash to the restroom to change.

While I'm waiting for a stall, I watch a woman with auburn hair working on a Sudoku puzzle. The man beside her nudges her and she studies the crossword clue he's working on. She frowns, then her brow softens and she fills in the squares.

"Not the Latin, they want the English," she says, watching him.

"Genius." He beams at her.

Maybe I could hand Devi's anagram over to this two-person brains trust.

When I return Rachel insists we swap seats so she can be a barrier between me and Libby. I snuggle into the window seat and smile at her.

"What's this?" Rachel bends down and scoops up the diary.

Shit. Has she looked inside it?

"Just a journal Mum gave me."

Rachel passes it to me, puts her headphones on and starts a movie.

I peel the sticky pages apart. Oma's photo is OK but the Coke has left an inkblot-shaped stain and the entry I was reading is ruined. The stain has soaked through layers and letters swim in an indecipherable mess. I kick myself for not making a copy of the diary before we left and keep turning the unreadable pages until I find a clean entry again.

The Behavioral Contract isn't worth the paper it was written on. Libby hasn't finished with me – it was all an act to make sure she could go on the trip. She didn't even wait until we landed to get her claws out.

The window cools my cheek. I close my eyes and try to relax, but I've screwed up big time. If – no *when* – I return the diary, now Stokes will know someone took it.

Good going, Mel. Real great.

Rachel positions her arm to shield her tablet from me: must be a sex scene. I flick back through the diary. There's a splash of Coke on one of the pages with an <u>E</u>. Thank God I wrote it all down in my notebook.

Devi, what the hell are you trying to tell me?

I check the other pages and my heart skips a beat. There's a clump of four pages with underlined letters, then a one-page gap with nothing underlined. Then it starts again for two pages, then a one-page gap. Then five pages with underlined letters, then another one-page gap . . .

Word puzzles. Charades.

The gaps must be for the end of a word, like a space. My heart beats YES and my pen flies to my notebook and I write down the letters, this time with the gaps.

EPHL EM REETH GGINO OT LIKL EM NI REEH

Come on, I've got this. I stare at EPHL but I can't make anything out of it. I tap my pen against my notebook and groan.

What am I missing?

All those times Ibu nagged us to learn more vocab. Damn.

There's something just out of reach, coming closer.

Crosswords. Brains trust. Genius.

Not the Latin . . .

Why I couldn't see it before? The letters weren't silent, they were shouting at me. In English. In a flying rush I crack the first word: *Help.*

I grin at my notebook.

I crack the next and something grips my throat.

Help me.

EIGHT

Devi's message is burning through me. Warping and twisting and turning everything sideways. No matter how many times I check and redo her anagram – could it be another word? Maybe I copied it down wrong? – I end up in the same squirmy place.

Help me they're going to kill me in here.

What do I do with that, Devi?

Tell me?

I've combed through the entries I've translated but I can't find anything that explains her message. Her parents sound like tyrants, but not killers. Not even close.

Rache giggles at her screen, eyes shiny. Should I tell her about this? I take a deep breath and look away. Rache is so perceptive I've never been able to lie to her outright. But I've avoided telling her things. Big time. She's got no clue about the Year I Stuffed Up. If I tell her about the diary she'll realize I'm capable of stealing from Stokes and then she'll start to question everything.

I grip my pen again and open the diary to the next unstained entry.

12 November

No Budi tonight. AGAIN. I waited for him, listened for his feet in the grass, but it was just me and the geckos. I tried to read but all the poems were sad ones. I sang instead and tried out a new song I wrote.

Why didn't he come?

His dove is still under my bed, surrounded by dust balls.

Earlier Mum and Dad were whispering. Dad's leg hasn't healed and the doctor won't allow him to work. His compensation runs out at the end of the year. Mum's going back to her village to ask for help. She's been working extra hours at the hotel for months, but this is serious.

Tonight I climbed higher than I ever have, but I couldn't escape a fear. It followed me when I left the house, like a bad spirit had hitched a ride on my shadow. Will they take me out of school before I can audition for Bandung? Will they make me work?

My dreams drop like vegetable peelings on the kitchen floor. They curl up and wait to be swept away.

13 November

No Budi.

14 November

In January it's my sixteenth birthday and most girls leave school once they turn sixteen. If they pull me out of school, I'll run away.

15 November

Lily's entering *Indonesia's Next Big Thing*, she's going to sing hip hop. If she can do it, maybe it's time I sang for a real audience, not just geckos. She says we could catch the bus there from school. Five days to decide. Tonight I tried out my song again, but I sounded flat and couldn't tune in. I read a little but my eyes kept drifting away from the page.

I used to be happy alone in my tree but now it feels strange. It's all Budi's fault.

Devi's life does my head in. After all my stuff-ups I'm shit-scared of being sent to Rokesby, but I've never had to worry about getting an education. My parents would freak if I didn't finish school and go to uni. I mean, every kid has a right to go to school.

Apart from the school stuff, there's nothing menacing. Maybe this is a prank, a trap to freak out diary snoops like me. But when I re-read her words – *Help me they're going to kill me in here* – my chest tightens.

I've got to work faster. Because I know in my bones that I haven't reached the bad part yet.

NINE

We squeeze into the arrivals hall at Jakarta's Soekarno-Hatta Airport with a mass of jostling passengers and struggle to stay upright. Taxi drivers strain against the barriers and yell, *Missus, missus! Taksi? Taksi?* Families sift through faces for their loved ones. Hotel staff wave signs and I giggle when I spot "Cheesum School" written in thick black letters.

Our bus driver hangs his arm over the barrier, removes a cigarette stub from his mouth and smiles at us, flashing small, neat teeth. He's tiny but he manages to shove a pushy taxi driver away from us and leads us outside to the sticky heat of the car park. The smell of cigarettes, sweat, and hot asphalt hangs in the air. We pile into the hotel bus and Ibu Sujati begins her headcount. With a nod from her, the driver fires up the bus, turns the A/C to deep freeze, and hits the highway with jangly music playing.

The silhouettes of palm trees, motorcyclists, and shacks flash by, before the scene becomes more urban. Construction cranes hang their heads. The call to prayer echoes from neighborhood mosques. Satay vendors fan their fires and people cluster on the streets to chat, laugh, eat, and play chess.

Our driver turns into a wide avenue and traffic banks up behind us. We're stuck like a fly in honey. I can't stop staring. Even through tinted windows, Jakarta infects me with its wired energy and for a few moments it pushes aside my panic about Devi.

With only two nights in Jakarta before we fly to Jogjakarta, we're expecting a lazy pit stop. All I want is to sleep in, lie around the hotel pool and translate the diary. But our chaperones are inhuman. They wake us at seven, give us half an hour at the buffet breakfast, then cram us on to a bus for endless excursions.

It's so frustrating.

We yawn non-stop on our visits to mosques and museums, but our tour of the old port of Sunda Kelapa shakes me awake. On the wharf wiry men with baked skin heave goods on to traditional wooden boats. They leer at us and the teachers hurry us along.

Our guide strides in front of us in khaki pants with

sharp creases and leads us to a slum by the water. The water is filthy with floating clots of scum and litter.

"I'm going to gag." Rachel pinches her nose.

The guide pulls a piece of tarpaulin aside and we enter. A smiling young mother emerges from one of the shelters, rocking her baby in a sling, and greets our guide. The woman's house is a patchwork of timber, garbage bags, and tarpaulin, with a sarong for a door.

The guide takes us past similar huts, all cramped together. Libby mutters snarky comments behind me, but I'm not playing. She caught me by surprise on the plane, but if this is her worst, bring it on.

Kids play on the flimsy pier, inches from the rank water. Chickens scratch around and a skinny goat is tied to the side of a home. The residents smile and say *hello missus* to us. I greet them, my smile tight. These are their homes and we're walking right through them. A teenage girl ducks out of her shelter and gives me a shy smile. She's attractive with alert brown eyes and soft black hair – a lot like Oma in her photo. For a moment I stand there blinking. Devi would be about her age too. I hope she isn't living like this.

What if she is? Her dad's not working so maybe things are really bad and they're starving? Or sick? That could be it.

They're going to kill me in here.

That doesn't sound like illness or starvation. Then she would have written: *I'm going to die in here.* I run my hands through my hair and frown.

Who are *they*, Devi?

I have to go faster. I'm pathetic – the other night I managed one line before I flaked out from exhaustion:

Budi's BACK. Too tired, write tomorrow.

"Are you OK?" Rache asks.

"Yeah. Just feel a bit sad."

She puts her arm around my shoulders, then immediately pulls away. "It's too hot for hugs."

I give her a weak smile.

By the end of the tour our group looks sick and grimy. The guide addresses us. Sujati and Kransky listen, their brows furrowed.

"People moved here after the government cleared their *kampung* to make way for a highway. They are proud people, but live in deep poverty. Anything you can give will help improve their lives." He holds out a jar for donations.

So that's why they're happy for us to stomp through their homes.

Libby pulls out a stack of notes. She waves her money in the air, passes it to the guide, then locks eyes with me and says, “I feel for people who have to live like this.”

Ibu Sujati falls for the Mother Teresa act and touches Libby’s hand. Is she gullible or what? Rachel shakes her head, but I’m still thinking of Devi and hoping it’s not as rough as this in her village – it must be better in the country. I grab a bundle of notes and shove them deep into the jar.

TEN

We're in Jogjakarta standing at the base of the Borobudur Temple. The afternoon sun glints on the ancient stone. I gaze up at the terraces and my heart takes flight.

"Kind of impressive." Rachel tugs her hair into a ponytail. Her hair has gone to shit here, with her curls turning to frizz.

"Yeah, they made an effort," I say.

The smoke from *kretek* clove cigarettes weaves around us as we climb up the stone steps. Sujati and Kransky are chaperoning the blonde girls in our group; Indonesian tourists are mobbing them like they're celebrities. Libby, with her blonde curls and long legs, is a prime target. At first she lapped it up but now she's trying to hide behind the petite Ibu Sujati. I can't stop sniggering and for once I'm happy with my brown hair.

"Hello, *turis*?" A long-haired Indonesian guy shadows us. He pulls his hair from his face.

Maybe this is karma, but something about his open face stops me from turning away.

"Yes, *turis*," I say.

"First time to Borobudur?"

We nod.

"I am Agus." He wears tight denims and a long-sleeved T-shirt but there's no sign of sweat on him.

We now have our own tour guide, whether we want him or not. A string of young boys trails after him, staring at us with wide eyes, then hiding behind each other.

Agus insists we walk in a clockwise direction to reach the first gallery. Relief sculptures tell a story on the stone walls. Beautiful goddesses dance, surrounded by worshippers and musicians. Warriors bare their teeth. Ships bob over rolling waves. Elephants lumber.

He points at a sculpture. "This story of Buddha." He traces his finger along the sculpture of Buddha in a cart, with a crowd of men and animals surrounding him.

"Should you be touching it?" Rachel says.

"This lava stone. Tough." Agus raps his knuckles against it.

We follow him through the galleries that cover the base of the monument. There are masses of tourists around us, above us, and beneath us, but for a moment I'm lost in the sculpture of the goddess in front of me;

I can almost see her eyelashes. Borobudur is massive but you need to get up close to find its beauty.

"Borobudur was hidden," Agus says.

"How could you hide this?" Rachel walks up to him.

"You know Merapi?"

"The volcano?" I say.

"Merapi – BANG!" He claps his hands. "Big explosion. Covered Borobudur in ash." He swings his arm wide, his *kretek* cigarette dropping ash.

"You're kidding?" Rachel says.

"They found again in the 1800s."

"Can you imagine stumbling into this? How incredible would that be?" I say to Rachel. But we were born too late to be explorers – there's nothing left to discover now.

After a lap of the temple we reach the top terraces. The teachers are still playing bodyguard to the blondes and keeping the rest of us in their peripheral vision. One of the little boys approaches Rachel and, ever the photo slut, she poses with him in a far corner of the terrace.

Agus beckons me with a flick of his wrist and ash floats down from his cigarette. He stands in front of a smooth-faced Buddha. It has hair like pineapple skin, drooping earlobes and a bell-shaped *stupa* that reaches to its shoulders.

Great, another bloody Buddha. My shoulders slump.

I'm covered in sweat and dust. How did I ever live in this heat?

"Put your hand through the hole and touch Buddha foot. Give good luck. Very lucky." Agus exhales smoke over his shoulder.

This is like one of those moments you see in the movies. I'll touch the Buddha, move a hidden wall, and reveal a forgotten kingdom, or have my hand caught in a barbaric booby trap and, years later, my cobwebbed skeleton will serve as a warning to other dumb tourists.

Agus jerks his head to one side, urging me on.

What the hell. I thread my hand through the diamond-shaped hole and reach until I'm up to my elbow and the little boys squeal. But my fingers wriggle in a void. I stretch further, until my fingers bend and bump into something fleshy. A snake? I shriek, yank my hand back and graze the underside of my arm on the stone. The boys hoot with laughter and clutch their sides.

The head of a teenage boy appears from the other side of the *stupa*. "Man, sorry about that." His messy black hair sticks out everywhere and his vivid blue eyes look like he's stuck his finger in an electrical socket. He unfolds his lanky body and stands up. "Wanted my bit of good luck."

"It's OK." I rub my stinging arm. "I didn't even get to touch it."

"Same." He shrugs. "We could have another go?"

"Let's do it," I say.

We step toward the *stupa* and pass our hands through the holes, careful to avoid each other this time. With my body pressed against the stone I wriggle my fingers and stretch until I think I'll dislocate my shoulder, but nothing. I reach a little further and touch a hard, grainy surface.

"I'm touching it." I grin at the guy. His cheek is squashed against the *stupa* and he's frowning.

"Me too." He smiles back.

Agus snaps us with my phone and the little boys run in front of us and stick their thumbs up in the air. We smile but floaters swim in my eyes. I'm up to my armpit in *stupa* with a strange boy beside me touching Buddha and wondering how luck will rub off from a foot that hasn't seen a pedicure in centuries.

When Agus hands me my phone we scroll through the images, with the boys hanging off us. Their tiny fingers leave prints all over the display. My hair's pasted on to my head, but I don't look too feral.

A hawker approaches and I buy drinks for everyone. I gulp down some mango juice and sneak a closer look at Buddha boy. He could be Indonesian with his dark skin and hair, but his blue eyes and height throw me.

We introduce ourselves and his name is Michael.

"Where you from?" I ask.

"Melbourne." He swats his hair out of his eyes.

"No way. Me too."

"You on holidays?" He drains his drink.

"Here with my school. You?"

"Catching up with relatives and doing a few side trips."

"Anywhere good?"

"Hope so. I want to go to Merapi, you know, the volcano?"

I hit the bottom of my drink and splutter. "You can go there?"

"It's been going off all week." He wipes his brow. "Don't want to miss the show. I'll try and go—"

Rachel bounds up to me. "There you are. I didn't see you behind that bell thing. Did you see? All these kids were taking my photo and I'm not even blonde. It's like having my own paparazzi."

"You'll get used to it." Michael swings forward from the wall and grins.

Rachel's eyebrows shoot up and I introduce them. Kransky's whistle cuts through the air. We barely have time to say goodbye before the teachers herd us back toward the bus.

That night in our hotel room the ceiling fan beats the thick air with *voom, vavoom, voom* swoops. Most nights Rache dives into the deepest fathoms of sleep while I find it hard to break the surface, but tonight she keeps twisting from side to side.

Come on, Rache. Please go to sleep.

The last two days have been torture. The teachers have driven us hard, filling every minute of the day, so I haven't had a chance to work on the diary.

Rache should be exhausted from ribbing me all night about Michael. I don't get what the big deal is. Hasn't she ever been friends with a guy? She's so into boys, but my time at Coburg Central convinced me that most of them are complete dickheads. The one exception was my mate Felix, but he's gay.

Like me, Jogja is wide awake. Outside, the cicadas' singing becomes frenzied. Street vendors' calls bounce back and forth across our narrow street. A man sings to himself. Rache is now deep under.

I slide out of bed and the sheet tangles around my ankle, but I save myself before I face plant. In the dark I grope for the diary and my torch, and creep back into bed. I fight my heavy eyelids and keep my back against the wall to stay awake.

30 November

Last night when Budi climbed up and pushed through the leaves all we could do was beam at each other. But then his smile dropped.

Budi went to Manado for his dad's memorial. His dad was a dive master who died in a freak accident a couple of months ago. After he told me his eyes were all shiny and he kept swallowing. He couldn't look at me. The gap between us felt huge. It would be horrible to lose my dad, even though he drives me crazy. I inched toward Budi and held his hand. We sat in silence and his hand felt soft and warm and perfect.

My eyelids flutter. Devi's world feels sweet and I want to stay there and slide into the dreaminess of her and Budi, but I can't stop yawning. What's so horrible about your life, Devi? It's way more romantic than mine.

1 December

Budi said scuba diving was like being an astronaut, but you float in water, not space. He made me shiver when he talked about thermoclines, these troughs where the seabed drops and the water is cold and hazy. Sharks lurk at the bottom of them. Ugh.

His stories remind me of how tiny my life is – this tree, school, home, the village. I haven't even been to Pineapple Village and nearly everyone at school has. It's so close. Will I ever go anywhere? I can't remember Sumatra. I was too young when we lived there and Mum and Dad won't talk about it. Too many sad memories. After the eruption we had to move to Java and we lost everything. They hate living so close to Merapi, it's a constant shadow for them.

After the eruption we had to move ... The back of my tongue tastes sour. Volcanoes are all about adventure for me, but for Devi's family a volcano was a disaster. I press my hands against the diary. It's not just their misfortune, I can feel the diary's secret growing and sometimes it's too much.

A rooster's high-pitched crow skewers my sleep. I fold my pillow over my ears but it's useless and Mr. Rooster is just getting started. With sleep-gunk in my eyes, I feel around on the floor for my phone and read the time. Four in the morning.

If I had a gun I'd shoot the little terrorist. I starfish on the bed and try to convince myself that I can nod off despite the crowing, but it's useless.

Rooster: 1. Mel: 0.

With a sigh I roll out of bed, grab my baseball cap, pull a top over my hideous bed T-shirt and slide into my flip-flops. I ease the door open and step out on to the balcony. Lime green geckos scurry across the wall. There's a courtyard below, lit with bamboo lamps and full of heliconia, bird of paradise, and ginger plants so lush they look like they're made of rubber. The windows above Ibu Sujati's and Kransky's rooms are dark and I tiptoe downstairs.

The reception and café are empty. Outside, most of the staff are near the front door in a cloud of *kretek* smoke, playing cards spread out on the ground with a pile of money in the center. They greet me and turn back to their game. Across the street my new friend, the *martabak manis* man, flips a pancake while a teenager waits on his silver scooter. *Martabak manis* man nods to me, his forehead shining with sweat. He wraps up the boy's pancake and then, without a word to me, prepares mine.

When it's ready I sit down on one of the plastic stools by his cart, swing my flip-flops from my toes and chew through the hot, sweet layers of pancake with its filling of chocolate and condensed milk. The street is bright with moonlight, and the smells of cloves, cinnamon, and ripe fruit mingle with barbecued meat.

There's a whoop from the card game and one of the players leaps up and thrusts his fist into the air. He bends down and scoops up his winnings. A few yards from them I spot a figure standing in a dark corner and, for a moment, a cigarette glows like a firefly in the dark and lights up her face.

It's Libby.

Her hand freezes but then she exhales again. I chew. She puffs and drags. We watch each other in silent challenge across the street. I could snitch on her, but by the time I reached the teachers Libby would be tucked up in bed, her mouth fresh with breath spray, and I'd have to explain why I'd snuck out.

She throws a butt on the ground and shoots me a final look before she strides back to the hotel.

ELEVEN

Our bus stops outside a white Dutch colonial building with an ornate wooden sign for the Wisma Language School hanging from the roof. We pad across spongy grass to a reception area. A petite young Indonesian woman greets us. Fine silver bangles slide down her wrists as she checks our names off a list and directs us to different classrooms.

Rachel and I enter Room Two. A man wipes down a whiteboard and writes his name in fat letters: PAK SUTOPO. His wrists are so delicate you could snap them like chicken bones.

I yawn and slump in my chair. Why do we have to ruin this trip with schoolwork? Then I think of Devi and her yearning to stay at school and I stop myself.

"That's my name. *Soo-toe-poh*." He rubs his hands and faces us. "This is the intermediate class so that means you're," he considers the six of us, "pretty good.

But at the end of your time here I want you to be brilliant. After this morning we'll only speak Indonesian in class."

Pak Sutopo reads my name tag. "Melati, could you open up that cupboard behind me?"

I swing open the heavy wooden doors. There's a wide-screen TV and a DVD player behind them.

"*Terima kasih*," Pak Sutopo says. He grabs the remote and hits the play button. "Welcome to a national obsession, the wonderful world of *sinetron*, or electronic cinema. I want a detailed plot summary at the end."

Sutopo hits play and the opening credits to *Jelita* roll. Glamorous Indonesian women with huge meringue hair swoon over buff Indonesian men. It's soap opera Indonesian-style, which seems just like the American version minus the sex.

I whisper to Rache, "I'm so stoked Libby's not in our class."

"I mean, they wouldn't want to risk throwing you two together, would they?"

"There'd be no need for *sinetron*, we'd have the Mel and Libby show instead."

Rachel snorts, Sutopo's eyes flicker toward us and we sink down into our chairs and stare at the screen.

Even after language school, an excursion to the Water Temple, and a massive meal, I'm too wired to sleep. An hour later I give up. Rache was envious when I told her about pigging out on *martabak manis*, so I whisper in her ear, "Rache, come out to play," but she's out. I grab the diary and slip out of the room.

Halfway down the stairs, I spot the poster: *Gunung Merapi – fire mountain. Take the night hike and witness one of Java's most spectacular volcanoes in action. Sign up here. Tours depart every night.*

The photos are thrilling – close-up shots of glowing lava pouring down the mountain and fireballs catapulting into the sky. The images pull me from the bottom of the staircase to the hotel's tours counter.

"Good tour, very excellent." The teenage boy behind the counter hands me a brochure. "It leave at midnight tonight and return at six in morning."

I pull at my bottom lip. It's after eleven now and everyone's sleeping. Maybe I could sneak out without anyone knowing. But I have to work on the diary. Devi's message is still haunting me and I'm no closer to finding out what's happened to her. It's been tough going – some sections of the diary are really difficult, and with our full-on schedule I hardly have any time for translating.

"You *berani*?" The boy behind the counter tilts his head to one side and grins at me.

"*Berani*?" I scratch my head. "Oh, brave! Yes, I'm very *berani*." I drum my chest like Tarzan to convince him and he giggles. "How *berani* do I need to be?"

"Oh, sometime is danger." He frowns and looks down at his paperwork.

"Good guides, ya?"

"The best."

"So, no problem?"

"No problem." He rubs his chin. "*Inshallah*."

People here say *Inshallah*, "God willing," all the time and it annoys me. This guy worries me – is it safe or not? And what am I thinking – Merapi is not on our itinerary. Ibu Sujati could never climb a mountain in kitten heels. Kransky could run up it backward with hand weights, but there's no way she'd take us close to a volcano. Maybe I could wake Rachel and convince her to come with me?

"You game?" a voice behind me asks.

It's Michael, the guy from Borobodur.

"Hello Pak Michael. Your forms are here." The guy passes Michael some paperwork.

"What are you doing here?" I say.

Good going, Mel. Real friendly.

Michael shifts his feet. "My cousin can't take me, but

he says this place does the best tours."

"I told you." The guy at the counter nods.

"Is that why you're here?" Michael tilts his head.

"I'm staying here. But I might . . ." I grip the edge of the counter and the diary digs into the inside of my arm. "I don't know."

"We leave in fifty minutes," counter guy says.

"You're going tonight?" I ask Michael.

"Yeah, I'm very *berani*." Michael grins at me.

My skin is all tingly. How long has he been standing there?

"Wouldn't miss it. There's a good chance of seeing lava." Michael grabs a pen and starts to sign the forms. There are heaps of liability clauses but the guy behind the counter doesn't ask Michael's age.

My body buzzes with the thrill of the forbidden. I hold on to the counter, swing back on my heels, and a distant warning sounds, but it's growing fainter and fainter. If the teachers find out I'll be on the next plane home.

Michael finishes signing and turns to me, his eyes bright. "You in?"

TWELVE

Our guides, Rusli and Amir, and their three mates wear scrappy flip-flops and lope along with perfect balance over loose rocks, uneven ground and a bitch of an incline. Steady streams of smoke trail behind them. I stumble in the dark in my sneakers, huffing and puffing. Michael is keeping up but he's used his inhaler a few times.

We're climbing a ladder to the stars in the Merapi sky. I'm grateful for the darkness; it stops everyone from seeing my heart-attack face. My legs burn and my breath turns into wheezes. I stop, lean into my thighs, and think of Rachel, tucked up in bed. It would be nice if she were here.

"Tough, ay?" says the Kiwi guy in our group of three. He's barrel-shaped and middle-aged but is taking the hike in his stride.

I catch my breath. "Maybe I shouldn't have done this after having the Jakarta squirts."

And maybe I shouldn't have said that out loud.

"That's hardcore." The Kiwi laughs.

"Not far," Rusli says. "Not far at all."

Rusli's a pathological liar; he's been saying that for at least an hour. We continue the climb and it's like one of those insane skyscraper stairwell marathons. Kransky would be proud if I wasn't breaking all the rules to be here.

The guides launch into a song and Michael joins in, but I don't recognize it.

"How do you know that?" A chunk of rock crumbles under my sneaker and I stumble.

Michael's arm shoots out to support me. "My cousin and his mates, we've been jamming. Don't understand the lyrics, not completely. Too much slang."

"What do you play?"

"Guitar, a bit. Can't sing for shit though." He smiles, then splutters and sucks hard on his inhaler.

"You OK?"

"Yeah." He tucks the inhaler into his jacket. "What got you interested in Indonesia?"

"Bandung. We lived there when I was little. So I guess I feel a connection. And my gran was Indonesian. I'm named after her."

"That's cool."

"Yeah, but she died when I was a kid."

"My dad's Australian, but Mum was Indonesian." He strides ahead of me. "How long were you in Bandung?"

I'm thrown by hearing him talk about his mum in the past tense. He tells me how his dad suggested the trip to get closer to his relatives and improve his Indonesian – he's doing classes at the local university. The chatter distracts us from the guides' unforgiving pace. The Kiwi troops on, sandwiched between us and the guides.

"Got any brothers or sisters?" Michael asks.

"One, Samuel. He's traveling around Australia getting over his broken heart." I slug down some water. "He's a total drama."

"Jack, my older bro, he's always heartbroken. Lives for it." Michael hauls himself up a steeper section and offers me his hand, but I pull myself up. "He always has a girlfriend."

"What about you?" My breath hitches. Uncomfortable seconds stretch between us and I'm glad he's in front of me so I can't see his face.

"Nah, I'm not like him. I don't need a girlfriend all the time."

"Yeah, know what you mean." But I'm a total fraud given my non-existent love life.

"You don't need a girlfriend?"

"I didn't mean, I meant—"

He shoots me a grin over his shoulder and I pull a face.

With one last giant stride, quads on fire, we reach the summit. It's so misty I nearly slam into Rusli. He gives me a thumbs up. "We stop now, Miss Melati. Wait for sunrise."

"Yes! Thank you!" I press my hands together and Rusli laughs.

Michael, the Kiwi and I look around for any sign of volcanic action.

"Is quiet now. You rest. Merapi is over there." He points into the distance at the foggy mountain next to ours. "You will hear when it wakes." Rusli guides me by the elbow to a makeshift hut and gives us blankets. His mates unroll some bamboo mats, stretch out, and fall asleep. The Kiwi joins them.

Now I'm at the summit there's no way I want to sleep. Michael and I stand in front of the hut, bounce from foot to foot and rub our arms, but the cold seeps through. We wrap ourselves in the blankets and stamp our feet, then dive back into the hut. The Kiwi blows out great snores and the rest of our group is a tangle of sleeping shapes. I shiver. I'm alone on a mountain with five guys. Strangers. What the hell am I doing?

The night yawns in front of us, a huge black void. There's nothing to hold on to with my eyes, unless I raise them to the stars. It makes me feel weightless, like I could float away. I dig my heels into the dirt and grip my blanket.

Michael and I mumble to each other from time to time, then sink into long silences. The wind whips at the entrance to the hut. I clench my jaw to stop my teeth from chattering and play with my peace ring. Is Merapi going to play tonight? I sneak a sideways look at Michael. He is staring into the darkness, still as a statue, his chin tilted toward his chest. I hug my knees and fold the warmth of the blankets around me.

"Miss Melati, Mister Michael, wake up. It begins."

My eyes snap open. Rusli is crouching in front of us, lighting a cigarette. Amir and his mates fold up their blankets and one of them prods the snoring Kiwi, who wakes with a snort.

"You are lucky, sometimes all this and nothing, or only at sunrise," Rusli says.

We stand up, stare into the darkness and stretch. Rusli holds up his hand and watches the groaning darkness, like a captain steering us toward land. We're all silent now. I tune in to the night and something catches in my throat when I hear it. It's faint, the barest of sounds, like a kettle warming up. Then the rumblings begin and start to roll in steadier waves. Merapi splutters, cracks and pops, a strange primal language.

As the lava rises the volcano spits and groans. A whiff of sulphur creeps around us, like smoke from a stick of incense. The first molten burst of lava catapults into the night sky, brands it with red-hot spray and splashes down the mountain with terrifying speed. It slows to a glowing, knotted rope. We whoop and I jump on the spot.

"Oh my God. Look at that," Michael says, his mouth open and his eyes on fire.

"Unbelievable." In the cold night, electricity fills my body.

More lava shoots out and chases the first molten rope, until the night is alive with smoke, and glowing rivers scar the mountain. Michael and the Kiwi's faces shine, lava reflected in their eyes.

On the way home in the taxi we talk non-stop, our heads close together. My skin buzzes with adrenaline. I should be wrecked but I can't stop smiling. I've achieved one of my ultimate fantasies of seeing a volcano in all its explosive glory. I've seen the earth's molten core, and I can't believe it. How many people experience that?

We turn into my street and our young driver pulls to a stop. We pay him, climb out of the car and turn to each other, not knowing how to end the night. It's like we're fellow travelers to a planet hardly anyone has visited.

"That was insane." My heart is singing.

The sun plays peek-a-boo with the horizon. I sway on the spot and Michael steadies me. After everything we've experienced his hand feels natural on my arm. On the front step we hesitate, then Michael holds the door open for me.

"You don't need to—"

"It's fine."

We enter and Libby's sitting in the café, propping her tired face over a cup of something hot, like she's trying to steam the bags away from under her eyes. I draw a finger to my lips and point to her. But I've forgotten about my sneakers, which squeak like hell on the tiled floor. Libby turns and spots us. She sculls her drink and takes off. We watch the waffled soles of her sneakers disappear up the stairs.

"Crap. She's heading straight for the teachers' rooms," I say.

"What a snitch." He pulls a face.

I laugh, but I've screwed up. Majorly.

THIRTEEN

Fifteen pairs of eyes stare at me when I arrive at breakfast late. My eyes are scratchy and I can't stop yawning. I head straight for Rachel at the buffet table. She smirks at me, then turns back to the breakfast buffet. I take a bowl of steaming *bubur ayam*, or chicken rice porridge, and spoon *kecap manis* on top. But I skip the deadly prawn crackers.

"Looks like vomit." Rachel grimaces.

"Don't care. I'm addicted to this stuff."

I place my bowl on a table far away from Libby and sink into the chair. "Oh my God." I grip my thighs but manage to sit down.

"A Merapi injury?"

"My quads. How am I going to use the squat toilets? I'll need a ladder or suction cups on the wall to help me down."

"Thanks for that visual." Rachel screws up her face.

I spear my first juicy morsel of chicken in rice gloop.

"I can't believe you snuck off like that." Rachel shakes her head.

"I tried to wake you to drag you along, but you were dead." I clear my throat. "Does everyone know?"

"Are you serious? You're lucky the wi-fi's down or everyone back home would know too."

She wriggles closer. "Everyone's saying you've been expelled."

"Nope. But I'm in the shit, big time."

"So what happened?"

After Libby snitched my first thought had been to deny everything because she'd only seen me talking to Michael. But once Kransky spotted my mud-caked sneakers I knew it was useless.

"House arrest," I whisper.

"Huh? What?"

"No excursions for me after class and they're giving me extra work. It was that or catch the next plane home." I swallow more porridge but it isn't sliding down so well.

"Are you serious?"

"Yup. Academic probation. Strike two. I'll have to study like crazy from now on or I could be suspended. Or worse." I give up on eating and my spoon drowns in the porridge.

“Don’t get expelled.” Rachel prods her eggs with her fork and blinks fast.

She’s tearing up. My throat tightens. My birthmark doesn’t lie; I’m a bad person and an idiot. I must be, only an idiot would get themselves into this mess. My heart feels heavy when I remember Ibu Sujati’s reaction: “You’re my star student. I pushed very hard for you to be allowed on this trip. Don’t make it a mistake.” That was news to me and I hated letting her down.

“So was Merapi worth it?” Rachel says to her eggs.

“It was pretty amazing.” I keep my eyes down too.

Last night the threat of losing my scholarship was no match for the pull of Merapi, but now my Merapi high is crashing big time.

My first session of hotel arrest isn’t tragic. The worst thing is Libby’s sneer from the back window of the bus as they take off. But I can stand missing out on stupid excursions to the Kraton, the Royal Palace, if I don’t have to cope with Libby’s smug face all afternoon. I should have snitched on her for smoking while I had the chance.

Idiot, Mel. Idiot.

Ibu Sujati and I walk back to the hotel. I’m about to climb the stairs to my room, when Sujati tilts her head toward the hotel café. "I need some tea and you can work in there."

I follow her. She sits down at one end of a long communal table in the middle of the cafe. I dump my books at the other end and sink into a cane chair. Sujati smiles at me and pulls out her tablet.

My phone beeps with a message: *Heard the news. Extremely disappointed in you. Please do everything the teachers ask and don't make things any worse. We'll talk when you get home. Mum.*

Could have been worse. When I shove my phone aside I catch Sujati watching me. I spread my homework out in front of me and get to work.

A waiter appears beside me holding a steel jug. "Coffee?"

"Yes. *Terima kasih.*" Because I'm such a crap sleeper I usually avoid coffee, but today I'm going to slug it down and power through the extra homework Pak Sutopo gave as part of my punishment.

"You are grounded?" the waiter says.

"How do you know?" I read the gold name badge on his chest. "Arief?"

"Your teacher?" He glances at Sujati, who is talking to someone on her phone.

I nod.

He fills my cup.

"Kraton is boring, that is why your teacher doesn't go. Only good if you like gamelan music."

"Sounds like tinny clanging to me." I screw up my nose.

"You insult Javanese music. I am offended." He presses a hand to his chest.

"Sorry, I didn't—"

He laughs. "I don't like it, but all the tourists go. I like better to stay here, drink coffee, smoke. Listen to Bob Marley."

"Sounds good, but no smoking for me."

"Yes, would be more trouble for you." Arief turns away to greet another customer.

Sujati's going to check my homework before dinner, but I've raced through it already. She's reading something on her tablet and sipping another cup of sweet tea. I slip the diary from my bag and hide it inside one of my school exercise books. If I'm careful, I can work on the diary during my hotel arrest. No more waiting for Rache to fall asleep and working by torchlight before I pass out.

"I will crack you," I whisper to the diary, and Oma's photo smiles back at me. The mystery of Devi's coded message has been keeping me awake at night.

18 December

Tonight was magic. I can't believe it!!! I'm so glad I entered. There's no way I'll sleep, I'm too excited. My voice and my legs shook like crazy at first, but as I sang and hit all the notes I started to fly. Lights danced over the audience – Budi, Lily, Detty, and other friends from school squealing at the front and jostling Ibu Yuliana. Dad talking to a woman, a stranger. When I reached for that top note and hit it, I swung on a rainbow.

Ibu Yuliana said winning second prize will help with my audition for Bandung. Budi said I was robbed but I'm too happy to care. My face is sore from smiling. I wasn't crazy to dream – they loved me.

It's a shock when the girls file out of the banana bus and into the hotel. I long to stay in Devi's world a bit longer; today it's sweeter than mine. Rachel sails past with Jasmine Saunders. I dive back into the diary.

19 December

Every night we reach the tree earlier and earlier. We sit closer and closer. I'm NOT imagining it. ♥

20 December

When I came home from school I could hear three voices behind a closed door – Mum's, Dad's, and another woman's – but not their words. It made the back of my neck prickle. They were still talking when I left.

Budi asked if it was something to do with my dad's leg, but I don't know. I just knew something was wrong. He fooled around after that, trying to cheer me up, hanging upside down from the higher branches and swinging in front of me. I warned him to stop and then he started to fall, but I grabbed him and he collapsed on to the branch, half-squashing me. We lay there for a moment. He must have heard my heart because it was pounding like crazy. He pulled away and we snuck glances at each other and I couldn't stand it anymore. We kissed, we finally kissed.

I could die with happiness. This is the best week ever.

My heart does a little dance for Devi. I wish I could do romance like her, but I've never felt like that about anyone. According to Rachel it's not in my DNA. With a dreamy sigh I close the diary.

That night Rachel turns on the lights to our room and three geckos fall from the ceiling and scamper away. We laugh our heads off.

Rachel pinches my arm.

"Ow! What the hell?" I rub at the nipped skin.

"Just checking." She sits down on the edge of her bed and stares at me. "What have you done with my best friend?"

I laugh, but a vertical frown appears between her eyebrows.

"You never used to get into fights and now you're sneaking out with random boys to climb volcanoes."

I arrange the mass of pillows against my headboard, leaving the sausage-shaped *guling* pillow to snuggle up to. "You're acting like Mum."

Rachel reddens. "Last year you were a goodie two-shoes."

"Gee thanks." I wriggle and a pillow tumbles.

"Well, you kind of were."

"I wasn't exactly . . . me."

Rachel tilts her head to one side, her eyes trained on me.

"Moving to Chis was a shock." I hug the *guling* pillow to me. "I tried to fit in but I hated being so fake. When that stuff happened with Grace I just couldn't stand Libby's crap anymore."

"And Merapi?" Rachel says.

"It was dumb, but volcanoes have always fascinated me, ever since Dad took me to Mount Bromo as a kid. And after all the shit I got for trying to help Grace . . ."

"Why do the right thing?"

"Yeah. What are we here for? To eat *nasi goreng*? I don't think so."

Rachel nods but she's still frowning.

"But that's it, I'll be a model student from now on," I say.

"Must be Multiple Personality Disorder. I've seen kick-ass Mel, goodie two-shoes Mel and—" Rachel counts on her fingers.

She doesn't see the pillow coming.

"Ahh! That's kick-ass Mel." She launches a pillow back at me.

I return fire.

Rachel ducks. "So Multiple Personality Disorder doesn't bother you but calling you a goodie two-shoes tips you over the edge?"

I sway to avoid Rachel's second pillow.

"So, this Michael guy, do you like him?"

My next pillow crashes into the cane lamp beside her.

"Ooh, violence. Must be serious—"

Armed with a pillow, I leap on to her bed to smother her. She squeals and kicks out. Someone bangs on an adjoining wall. I turn out the lights to prevent a counterattack and belly flop on to my bed.

In the dark my secrets queue up on the tip of my tongue. They're waiting to leap, but I press my fist against my lips. The room is silent apart from the rattle of the ceiling fan, until Rachel speaks.

"You're a mysterious creature, Melati Nelson. Just when I thought I'd figured you out."

FOURTEEN

Pak Sutopo is at the whiteboard, writing. When he's finished he spins around and takes a step to the side. He's written "*DANGDUT*" in proud letters on the whiteboard. The word teases me. I squint and try to work out why I recognize it.

He props himself against the front of the desk. "Have any of you heard of *dangdut*?"

The others shake their heads and then it hits me.

"It's a type of music, popular music," I say.

He beams at me. "That's right, Melati. Very good."

It's Devi's music.

When the bus drops me off at the hotel, I feel a pang – they're seeing a *dangdut* performance after class. I'd love to experience *dangdut* for myself. It would make me feel closer to Devi and her dreams.

Ibu Sujati escorts me to the café where a young woman

with silver bangles piled around her wrists is waiting for us by the door. She looks familiar.

"Melati, this is Citra from the language school. She's going to be supervising your detention," Sujati says.

Citra gives me a big smile. While they talk in hushed voices, I spread out my things at the same spot as yesterday and start my obedient student act. After Sujati leaves, Citra sits at a nearby table for two and pulls out a fat textbook.

"Anatomy," she says, without looking up. "I'm going to be a physiotherapist."

"Cool. Are you a teacher at the school?"

"No, a tutor and I help with the front desk."

While I'm working through my homework, I plug in my earbuds and find a *dangdut* song on my phone. An old memory prods me – Oma used to dance around the house to music like this. I smile and keep listening, picturing her whirling around the kitchen, me and Samuel bopping and laughing beside her.

I pull the diary from my bag. Today I'm going to solve the riddle; my bet is that Devi's parents are abusing her and it's got something to do with Budi.

Arief pours me more coffee. "No homework today?" He points at the diary. "You are too interested. Even when the others return you work hard on it."

I press my index finger to my lips and glance at Citra. He shrugs, leaves a bowl of nuts on my table and leaves.

He's right, I've still got homework to finish.

Citra stands up and slings her handbag over her shoulder. "Five minutes," she says, and wanders out to the café's garden area. Between the gaps in the white lattice wall I watch her light up.

Someone taps me on the shoulder and I jump. It's Michael.

"Sorry. What's up?" He pulls up a chair opposite me. Michael's wearing rainbow-striped pants and a batik shirt. It's kind of hideous but he pulls it off with his I-don't-give-a-crap attitude. Without thinking I close the diary.

"Hello there." I smile at him.

Michael rubs the back of his neck. "I hope I didn't get you into trouble the other night. Coming in with you and everything. I should have—"

"Nah, I'm the one who snuck out." I fiddle with a teaspoon and tell him about my punishment and Citra. "It was worth it though."

We grin at each other.

"Yeah, it was crazy. Beats any school excursion. How's your detention going?" He rests his forearms on the table.

"They're giving me stacks of homework but I'm speeding through it." I pull the diary back toward me.

Michael glances at it. “Who’s that?”

Oma’s photo has fallen out from under the cover.

“My gran.”

“You look a little bit like her.”

“Can I tell you a secret?” I press my palm against the cover of the diary and launch into the story of Devi. “It’s like she was trying to cry out for help without the wrong people finding out about it. I’ve been translating it but it makes no sense. There’s no danger yet. It’s driving me insane.”

“Maybe she’s making it up?”

The thought isn’t new but I know Devi’s not faking it. “What if it’s real? I’m getting faster but I’m too slow. What if she’s in real danger but it’s too late by the time I translate it all?”

“I could help? We could split it between us?”

“You’d do that?”

“Sure.”

I want to hug him, but I shout him a coffee instead.

Michael races to the print shop and makes a copy. When he returns I motion toward Citra, who is bent over her textbook. He sits down on the other side of the communal table, within whispering distance, and starts to scan through some of my translation.

"You know, I'm getting the same as you. Pretty much," he whispers.

"Great." My shoulders unlock. I hadn't even realized I was tense.

I divide up the remaining diary entries, sneak a look at Citra, and push his pile across the table.

"I'll keep working on it," he says.

Citra strides over, stands right beside me. "Everything OK?"

Shit.

"All good." I force a smile. "Citra, this is Michael, a friend I ran into from Melbourne. He was helping me with a passage I was stuck on."

Michael reaches out his hand and shakes hers.

"Finished?" She points to the jumble of papers on the table.

"Nearly. Do you want to check it?" I show her the exercises I did earlier and she scans them.

Citra looks from me to Michael. "Is OK, but don't talk too much." She hands my homework back. "Sujati said she'll check your homework each night. I just make sure you do it."

We wait for her next cigarette break before speaking again.

"I'm checking out this punk band tonight with my

cousin. Want to come?" Michael pulls at the multicolored braid around his wrist.

I sag against my chair. "I'd love to but I can't risk it."

"No problem. I'd better go, looks like your group's back."

Sure enough the bus has pulled up outside the front door. Michael is halfway out the café's side exit as Chis girls loaded with shopping bags step down from the bus.

The next day I rush to the café and Michael's already there with his papers on the table. Arief has my coffee ready. Got to love these two.

"How was the band?" I slide into a chair on the same side of the table as him.

"Hilarious. The singer kept diving into the crowd. Backward. The guitarist blew up an amp and then kicked it off the stage."

"Sounds cool."

I open my homework and get started. Citra rushes in, waves at us with her bangles jangling and sits down at the same table as yesterday. Arief flies over to her with a mug of ginger tea.

While Citra and Arief are chatting, Michael slides his translation across to me. My face lights up – he's done so much. I pass my section to him and we start reading.

3 January

I hate my life. Hate it, hate it, hate it.

Mum has ruined everything. Budi and I were in our tree when she snuck up on us and yelled at me to come home. She was standing in the shadows beneath us, her arms folded, her face mean. Budi and I jumped apart. We climbed down and poor Budi tried to introduce himself, but she wouldn't even look at him. So rude.

She dragged me up the path and hurled questions at me about Budi. I tripped and yelled that she was hurting me. She roared back that I better not shame the family.

Mum talked about the neighbors, about people noticing me sneaking off to meet a boy. I stomped my foot and yelled that it was none of their business and that I wasn't doing anything wrong. I told her I did everything she asked, but she still treated me like a servant, not a daughter.

She crumpled a bit then. She asked if Budi was Christian – like that matters – and I said how much I liked him, just to anger her. But she said I was a child who didn't know what I was talking about.

If I'm a child, why does she make me work like an adult? It's so unfair. She's a monster.

I glance at Citra. She's chewing on her pen, frowning over her anatomy textbook and writing notes. My homework is looming over me so I return to it and don't let myself read any more of the diary until I've almost finished my work.

5 January

My parents are my jailers. Except when I'm at school, I'm a prisoner. Every night they pile on the chores and I can't study. They know how important my marks are for the audition, but do they care? NO. They want me to fail, drop out and get a job. All they care about is money, but I'm not giving up. I won't be their slave.

Michael passes me a note. *See where she talks about being their slave? Maybe that's what the coded message is about – they're killing her with work?* He looks up at me.

I reread the passage. "I don't think so," I whisper.

Worse still, I haven't seen Budi. I tried to sneak out but they stopped me. I miss him so much. He must feel it. My heart beats out smoke signals. I look into the sky for his return signals, but the sky is empty.

6 January

When I arrived ~~home~~ at my prison, a delicious smell carried me to the kitchen. A bubbling wok of chicken curry. Dad's work friend, Ibu Sri, brought it round. I wanted to cry. I didn't have to cook dinner for once and we hadn't eaten meat for weeks. Ibu Sri, thank you, thank you, thank you.

After dinner the little ones and Dad drifted off to sleep. I watched their faces. Rusli's pudgy cheeks, his mouth open, Dini and Inan curled up like kittens. Dad's floppy hair tickling his nostrils when he snored. They tugged at my heart. I do love them, but I hate being poor. I hate being the eldest. I hate this village.

Mum was still at work, so I snuck out and ran to my tree, but it was empty.

7 January

I'm so upset I can't even write down what happened. It makes it too real. Life is terrible. Happy birthday? This is the worst one I've ever had. Please give me another life.

9 January

What did my loving parents give me for my birthday? A job. Dad's colleague from the factory, Ibu Sri, found me one. I knew her chicken curry was too good to be true. I should have spat it out.

Mum and Dad accepted without even asking me. They sat me down and told me about a "brilliant opportunity" to work for a year as a nanny for a businessman and his two small children.

The job's in Melbourne, Australia. When Dad told me I couldn't speak. I was too busy screaming inside. They smiled, they actually smiled, and waited for me to say something, like I should be happy about it.

I said, *No way. I'm not going, you can't make me.*

Mum tried to hold my hand, said it was only for a year and then I could come back to school. Dad told me the money I'd earn in Australia would make a big difference. I told them I wanted to stay in school and audition next year and that I didn't want to leave the family. I begged them to let me find some part-time work here instead. My hands shook so hard I had to hide them under the table. I felt cold all over, I still do.

Dad got teary and said he didn't want to send me so far away, he loved me, but they couldn't make it on their own. He asked me if I thought Irianto had wanted to leave school and send us nearly everything he earned. His eyes burned into me until I had to look away.

When I think of Dad's leg I want to tear this diary apart. I want to scream at Ibu Yuliana for ever letting me dream.

Citra shuffles out on her wedges to the garden for a smoke.

Michael's eyes shift between my translation and the diary. "She must have come to Australia, that must be how the diary ended up in Melbourne."

Uh oh. I know what's coming. I fiddle with my peace ring.

"Where did you find it, anyway?"

I keep my eyes down as I tell him.

"Oh, man. You're bad." He elbows me in the ribs. "But the school counselor? Why the hell did he have it?"

"Don't know." I shrug. "It's not like I can ask him, not if I want to keep my scholarship."

I grab the diary and find the entry we were reading. The next entry is weeks later – 15 March. It's weird though, her handwriting's different. It's suddenly spidery, cramped. Like she's trying to hide. The bus will be back in minutes but I keep going.

15 March

Night is the worst time. The blue glow sneaks in around the edges of the window. The window is painted over, except at the top where there's a small gap. If I stand on tiptoes I can see a green vine, a silver tree, red brick and a triangle of sky.

Why do I bother to look? It does no good. No one knows where I am.

The street is so quiet it terrifies me. There are no arrows on the ceiling, so I don't know which way to pray. But I pray like mad. I want to write down what's happening but I'm scared the shame will destroy me. But if I don't write, I'll go mad.

I am *ayam potong.*

"*Ayam potong* means 'chopped chicken', right? How could she be chopped chicken? Am I missing something?" I stab the tip of my pen into my notebook.

"That's weird." His arm presses against mine as he reads the passage. He searches through the dictionary then snaps it shut. "I've got nothing."

Heavy brakes groan out the front and seconds later I hear Ibu Sujati's voice.

"Crap." She'll want to check my homework soon.

"Better run." Michael grabs his stuff, his hand lingering

on my arm. "I've got this family dinner tonight but I'll try to keep going." He shoots out the door.

Citra enters and whinges about her upcoming exam. I smile and turn back to my homework. Rachel and Jasmine appear in the doorway.

"There you are." Rache holds up a shopping bag. "We've got something for you."

I'm so close to Devi's secret I can taste it.

FIFTEEN

Pak Sutopo prowls, doing laps from the whiteboard to the window and back to his desk. The fan whirls overhead, shooting little bursts of cool air down my arms. We groaned when he hit us with this surprise test but I'm breezing through it.

Time's up and I'm the first to hand it in.

"Melati, can you stay behind for a minute, please?" Pak Sutopo says.

Rache gives me a pained look and slips past me.

Pak Sutopo looks down at his pile of marking and waits until everyone has left before meeting my eyes. "Melati, you've improved so much. But you're behind on your homework. You were doing so well there to begin with, what happened?"

For the first few nights of my hotel arrest Sujati had checked my homework. Then she'd left it to Sutopo.

"Sorry, I got caught up reading something else and

underestimated the time I needed."

"Your teachers asked me to track your work closely. I want to be flexible because you're doing so well, but I can only give you another day to catch up."

"I'll do it tonight. Promise."

"Fine. See you tomorrow."

I hesitate.

"What is it?"

"Um, *Bapak*, I was reading something and I didn't know what it meant." My mouth dries out.

"Go on."

"What does *ayam potong* mean? I know it means chopped chicken, but does it have another meaning?"

His face stiffens. "Like you said, it means chopped chicken."

"But what if a person says they are *ayam potong*?" I chew my bottom lip.

"Where did you read that?"

"In a blog."

He twists the lid of his fountain pen back and forth and considers me. "You shouldn't be reading blogs like that." He pulls one of the exams toward him and starts marking.

I can't forget the look on Pak Sutopo's face, like I was a war criminal or something.

What had I said to him?

In the café, Arief nods to me. He's waiting on guests who are taking forever to order. He sneaks a secret eye roll my way and I hide a laugh behind my hand. Citra is messaging someone on her phone, her pink fingernail tapping across the screen. There's no sign of Michael. I open the diary, reread the *ayam potong* entry and sigh. Arief approaches with coffee – I'm about to ask him but I back out. What if he gives me the same look as Sutopo? I turn the page.

19 March

Sometimes when I wake up I forget for a moment. Then I remember and I can't breathe. I sob until I think I'll choke. The pain covers me like a lead blanket, presses down on me until I'm sure I'm going to die.

It's better never to forget. That's why I have to write this down.

The first time they drugged me. I struggled to open my eyes. The fog cleared and a stranger was on top of me. My limbs were weak, it was like fighting my way out of a pit of rice. His mouth sealed mine and I couldn't scream. The drugs clouded my mind, then cleared again and made the horror unbearable. I shut my eyes and prayed to pass out, but his movement kept throwing me back into my body. On the ceiling a spider with long skinny legs spun a web. I watched that spider, hung on to it like a lifeline.

After he finished, shame skimmed across his face. He stood up, hauled his belly back into his pants, tucked his shirt in and fixed his tie. Was he going back to work? To his family? He looked ordinary.

When I came to, Kurt was sitting on my bed. His bulk and the tight blanket trapped me. He waited until I was fully awake and tapped a yellow envelope against his knee. His blue stare chilled me. He wrote on the envelope: $30,000. Kurt pointed to me, then rubbed his fingertips together. He opened the envelope and pulled out photos of Mum, Dad, the kids flying a kite, even Budi.

How did Kurt have them?

Ibu Sri.

I remembered her talking to Dad at the talent quest. That must have been when she first saw me and made me her prey.

Kurt grabbed my cheeks and forced me to smile. He spoke to me like I was an idiot, his dirty blond hair hanging over his eyes. "You will make happy, yes? Or . . ." He pointed to the photos and dragged a finger across his throat.

I wanted to gouge his eyes out. But I knew I was trapped. Kurt grabbed the back of my head, forced me to nod, again and again, until I begged him to stop.

SIXTEEN

It can't be. I stare at the words on the page. They've leaped from the diary and grabbed me by the throat. Questions fly at me, stinging me like I've disturbed a nest of wasps.

"Melati? No problem, is OK?" Arief frowns at me.

"My stomach's funny."

Arief disappears behind the kitchen door and returns with a big mug. "Ginger tea. It make you better."

I thank him and grab the pages again, flicking through the remaining entries with shaking hands. There are rushed pages where the dates disappear, like a prisoner who has stopped marking time. I've always wrestled with feeling like an intruder when I've been reading her diary; now it's so much worse. But I have to keep going and find out if she's still trapped. I skim ahead. There are nights of horror. And fear. Fear soaking deep into every page.

Then a spark of hope when she meets a new client.

Mr. Gerald seems kind, better than the others. When he spoke Indonesian to me, I almost died on the spot. If he returns I'll try to get him alone and ask him for help. I know he'll help me.

I skim ahead to the last entry.

23 March

Ewa's bed is still empty. None of us have seen her for days. We're all terrified, we all heard her fight with Kurt.

When Mariska said Mr. Gerald was a good man, I dared to hope, but hope is poison. He hasn't come back. Even if he does it's too risky to tell him. If Kurt found out he'd kill me. I have to find another way.

I pray that Kurt lets me go when I've repaid my debt but it's so much money. I won't last that long. How will I ever go home? My family will be so ashamed. Budi won't want me now.

The waiting is the worst. Not knowing when someone is going to pick me. Not knowing if they'll be a disgusting pig or almost human. Not knowing what they'll ask me to do. Not knowing if I'll be able to hide in my head until it's over.

I feel young and stupid because I'd hoped, somehow, that Devi would be free by the last page. I guess I still believe in fairytales, but the world is trying to beat it out of me.

The pages fall open on the drawing of a man's face. I remember it from all those weeks ago, when I first took the diary. He could have been beautiful, but there's something a bit twisted about his features.

It's Kurt. It has to be. It matches her description of him.

I stumble over to Citra and tell her I need some air.

"Sure, no problem," she says. "I can see you from here."

Outside I sit on a cane chair, crouching behind the courtyard garden of palm fronds, ginger plants, and birds of paradise. The setting is so beautiful that it feels obscene compared to the ugliness of the diary. I don't have words for what's happening to Devi. On my phone I search for *sex work* and *rape*. Google spits out some feminist sites and some dodgy ones, but when I type *forced sex work* it leads me to *human trafficking*, where people are traded as slaves for forced sex work or other labor. The more I read, the sicker I feel. How can this exist in the world?

What if I'm wrong? I could be freaking out about nothing. I message Michael: *REALLY IMPORTANT.*

Check 19 March entry pls? Need another opinion.

The ginger tea hits the back of my throat and the sweet, spicy liquid washes away some of the dirty feeling, but then a new thought rises and a bolt of adrenaline surges through me.

What if I'm right?

SEVENTEEN

My phone glows with a message from Michael.

Downstairs.

Rache is facing the wall, her lungs rising and falling in long, deep breaths. Fully dressed, I rip the blanket back and jump out of bed. Outside on the balcony I glance at the windows above the teachers' rooms but all the lights are off. Barefoot, I power walk across the balcony and downstairs, my heart making a crazy beat in my chest.

Ever since I translated the entry it's been hell. Waiting for Michael to respond, doing a stack of homework so Sutopo doesn't out me, and having to act normal at dinner – when all I could think about was Devi.

I rush to the courtyard but I can't see Michael.

"Over here." A voice reaches me from my left.

Michael's standing in a shadowy corner behind some tall potted palms, like we're in a spy movie. For a moment

I'm about to laugh, then I think about what would happen if someone spotted me.

I step closer until I can see his face. One look at him and my heart's in my throat.

"This is heavy shit. She's like … a sex slave." He squeezes the bundle of pages. We sink into the cane chairs in the corner. "If it's true."

"You don't think it's made up?" My back stiffens. What if Stokes kept it because Libby or some disturbed student he'd counseled had written it?

Michael shakes his head. "Feels real, doesn't it?"

"Too real."

"It's disgusting. I can't believe people do this in Melbourne. I mean, it's so messed up." His eyes blaze. "We've got to do something."

Help me they're going to kill me in here.

"But what? We don't even know where she is."

Michael rifles through the pages to the final entry. "How long ago did you find it?"

"Um, let me check." I grab my phone and scroll through my calendar to my first session with Stokes. "Start of April."

"So, do you think …?" He gives me a guarded look.

"What?"

"Do you think she's still … alive?"

I stare at him.

"It's just, what she says about that other girl."

"Ewa?"

He nods.

If only my Indonesian was better. If only I'd cracked her message sooner.

"She has to be," I say.

I fiddle with my peace ring and am about to sacrifice my last chewable fingernail, when Michael says, "But the school counselor? Why the hell did he have it?"

"Don't know." I grimace.

Mum's always telling me not to jump to conclusions but horrible thoughts about Stokes are niggling me. But Stokes is a good guy. There must be a reasonable explanation.

"Does she mention him?"

I shake my head. We both slump against the wall.

"Maybe . . ." I push myself off the wall and turn to him.

"What is it?" His face is so close I can feel his breath.

"Maybe we can find her family. Or Ibu Yuliana."

EIGHTEEN

On the bus back from class Rache rests her cheek against my shoulder. "You look like a wreck. Your insomnia is out of control."

I rub my eyes. "I'm used to it."

After Michael left I snuck back to our room, but once I hit the mattress I couldn't stop thinking about Devi. From the bathroom I tried to call Dad but the line was crap, wherever he was, and he couldn't understand me. I tried again and it didn't even connect. Then I got up early to finish my homework for Pak Sutopo. All up I managed three hours' sleep.

"I don't know how you do it."

"Arief's coffee will keep me going."

Rache gives me a you're-a-mess-girl look.

The bus turns the corner into our street.

"Don't worry, the tea plantation will be crap."

According to Rache every excursion I've been banned

from has been crap. I wink at her and stumble down the aisle. The teachers avoid looking at me and I have to stop myself from running down the steps. All I want to do is figure out how to track down Devi.

Michael's already at our table with his notebooks and a steaming great mug of Arief's coffee in front of him. Our eyes meet and I rush over. "How long have you been here?"

"A while, thought I'd get a head start. Crack this case wide open."

"So have you?"

"Nope."

"Where's Citra?"

He shrugs and smokes an imaginary cigarette. But I can't spot her outside.

Arief approaches and asks if I want some ginger tea.

"Nah, need your coffee today."

Citra enters, barely nods at us, her hairline damp with sweat. Her hand slides to her stomach and she folds into her chair.

"*Sakit*?" Arief asks.

"You OK?" I ask.

"No." She grimaces and props her head in her hands. When Arief appears with ginger tea she grabs the mug, but after a few sips she bolts for the door.

"Poor Citra." I pull a face.

"We've all been there," Michael says.

Michael turns his notebook so I can see the mind map he's drawn with Devi in the center and two branches. One says *rural village* with stems for *factories (Dad)*, *fields*, *trees*, *Merapi* and *hotel (Mum)*. The other says *Christian college in the city (Budi)*.

"I'm making a note of anything that might pinpoint her location," he says.

We scan the diary for more clues. After one cup of coffee I add a third branch, *high school*, with a stem labeled *Ibu Yuliana* and another for *co-ed*. Michael adds *Java* next to the *rural village* branch.

"That narrows it down."

He shrugs.

We don't get any further with the map. I start my homework even though my temples are aching and my forehead feels tight. Maybe I need more than three hours' sleep.

Citra staggers back into the café. She braces herself against our table. "Melati, I must go. Is not good." She closes her eyes for a moment, her jaw tense. "I've called Sujati. She said for you to do homework until they return. I trust you?"

"Yeah, course. Do you want me to get you a taxi?"

Arief appears by her side. "I called one." He holds her elbow and guides her out the door.

Michael slides his hands into his pockets. "Want to go for a juice? They do the best soursop ones down the street."

The bus gets back in two hours. Plenty of time to do my homework.

"Why not? But it's my shout." I stand up and slip my arm into his.

Arief gives me a quick glance, but I've been working flat out and there's only so much I can take. Still, my teachers might not see it that way. What if they have Arief on their payroll? I leave him an extra big tip, just in case.

The café is a few blocks away in a cavernous shed with jungle vines growing over it. The soursop juice is luscious, like strawberry and pineapple mixed together with a hint of coconut ice cream.

"Haven't you had one before?" Michael says.

"Nope. Soursop, where have you been all my life?"

Michael snorts. He thinks I'm kidding.

We wander past the café, deeper into the shed, and I think of Citra. What if she comes back? But she looked so sick. A crackle of feedback from the back of the shed blasts my nervousness away.

"That's Yandra, my cousin."

Yandra's on the electric guitar, standing on a stage made of wooden crates. He swipes at the guitar, his blue-black hair standing on end. He spots Michael and a smiles flashes across his face.

A small crowd surges around us as a tiny singer with a microphone jumps up on to the crates. The ends of her dark braids are dyed red and skim her shoulders. With her skinny black-jeaned legs and her huge leaps across the stage she reminds me of a jumping spider – a very pretty one. When she starts to sing it's a huge, snarling death-metal roar.

She arches her back, grips the microphone like she's going to crush it and her monster growl keeps rolling and deepening and filling the space. She's channeling something primal and infernal and it's ugly and magnetic at the same time.

Michael slides into the mess of jumping bodies. He moves with the mass of dancers, his hair bouncing, eyes shut. In a trance. The singer growls again and the mosh pit accelerates, like charged particles. The ceiling fans are on full blast but they only poke at the heat. I gaze at the singer – how does a tiny, feminine woman channel so much rage? Was she born with it or did something happen to her? She's head to head with Yandra, screaming into the microphone. She'll never win a Grammy but she's amazing.

I think of Devi performing at the talent quest and her love of *dangdut*. Will she ever do that again? We've got to find her. But how? All we know is that she lived in Java in a village and went to high school until her family pulled her out. If only we could find her high school, but there are so many in Java. We've got nothing.

I step back from the crowd and tug the diary from my bag. Beneath the thud of drums and the singer's wild snarling growls, my heart pounds when I find the entry.

NINETEEN

15 November

Lily's entering *Indonesia's Next Big Thing*, she's going to sing hip hop. If she can do it maybe it's time I sang for a real audience, not just geckos. She says we could catch the bus there from school.

"What is it?" Michael's standing over me. He slides onto the bench next to me, his forehead wet. I catch a whiff of him.

"Man, you smell." I pull a face and push my hand out, aiming for his shoulder but my palm ends up stuck against his chest. His surprisingly firm chest. Our eyes meet and I snatch my hand away.

"Think I've found something. Devi performed in *Indonesia's Next Big Thing* on 18 December, right?"

He nods.

"She says she could catch the bus there from school.

If we find out where the talent quest was we've got a chance of finding her school."

His eyes light up and he grabs the diary. "She doesn't say where it was but they must've advertised it." He pulls out his phone and starts searching. His face falls.

"What?" I try to see the screen.

"They held three shows in Java on 18 December. Forget Jakarta, it's not exactly rural. That leaves Surabaya and Salatiga."

"How big's Surabaya?"

He types on his phone, squints at the screen and groans. "It's huge."

"And Salatiga?"

"Less than 200,000 people."

"Hmm, we'd have a chance with that."

"There's got to be something else."

Michael flicks through the entries – entries we've translated and read until we can see them inside out.

Yandra lopes up to us, his chest bare and his jeans glued to him. His hair's in tufted clumps, full of sweat and heat. He flashes me a big grin, flops beside me and introduces himself.

"That was . . . wild," I say.

"You've never seen Lina before?"

"Never seen anyone like her."

"She's a freak. We love her."

Michael frowns. "Ever heard of Pineapple Village?"

"Kampung Nanas? Sure. Tourist place. They painted all the houses orange and the roofs green to look like pineapples. It's kind of cool but sort of . . ." He inclines his head.

"Tacky?" I say.

"Yeah."

I glance at Michael. What's he getting at?

The alarm buzzes on my phone. I've got an hour and fifteen minutes before the bus rocks up. Just enough time to do my homework. I jump up and grab my stuff. "Got to get back."

"I'll walk you," Michael says.

The three of us head toward the door.

"So where's this village?" I ask.

"Don't tell me you want to go there?" Yandra jostles Michael.

Michael shrugs.

"It's two hours away. We could go on my bike. Not far from Salatiga," Yandra says.

"Salatiga?" My voice rises.

"Yeah. A real nothing town." Yandra holds the door open and I lock eyes with Michael. "But we can go if you want."

TWENTY

That night after dinner Kransky bangs her spoon against the side of a glass. "Girls, get a good night's sleep because it's an early wake-up tomorrow." She holds up a hand to silence our immediate groans.

"But it's the weekend," says one girl from the back of the room.

Her lips tighten. "You've experienced lots of Indonesian culture on our excursions—"

"Some of us have." Libby shoots me a glance.

Subtle, real subtle.

"We thought you might enjoy seeing some expatriate culture. So tomorrow you'll experience the Hash."

Kransky is taking us to smoke hash? Someone has messed with the order of the universe.

"But Miss, Mum warned me not to touch that stuff," Rachel says, smirking, and a few girls snigger.

"Very cute, Olliver. I'm not suggesting that you have

a bucket bong." Kransky smiles and Ibu Sujati frowns. "No, the Hash House Harriers have a long tradition here. It's a cross-country run—"

We all groan.

"Through countryside you'd never normally get to visit."

"Or would want to." Rachel shoves her plate away and drops her head to the table.

"We'll meet outside the hotel at six-thirty. That's the end of it." Kransky sits down.

"Sounds like hell. Can you imagine, in this heat?" Rachel dips her now rubbery prawn cracker into a puddle of sambal and offers me some.

I push the plate away. "You trying to poison me?"

She holds the prawn cracker aloft. "Shit, I forgot. But it'd get you out of the Hash."

"No need. I'm grounded, remember?" I smile, I'll have a whole day to find Devi.

"Mel, you'll join us for this one." Kransky's voice reaches us from the other side of the table.

"Seriously?" I scowl.

Rachel snorts behind her hand.

"Don't test me." Kransky walks away, no doubt to fit in some chin-ups before bed.

"I can't believe she said bucket bong. Maybe she's a closet pothead?" I say.

Rachel bites into her remaining prawn cracker. "Nah. Would stuff up her triathlon time."

Kransky bangs a gong outside our door. Rachel and I fall from our beds and stumble around looking for our gym gear. After Rachel had complained about the stench from my sneakers I'd left them outside to air for a couple of nights. I open our door, blink hard in the morning glare, grab a sneaker and slide my foot into it. But I can't shove my foot all the way in and the inner soles are kind of squelchy. My hand covers my mouth. Have I squashed some tropical insect with my toes? I pull my foot out and meaty chunks of black gunk, like scary bug entrails, cover my sock.

I sniff my shoe. It reeks of banana, fermenting banana. What the hell? I scoop out the chunks and throw them into a pot plant by the door.

Crap.

Rachel's in the bathroom brushing her teeth. I push past her to scrub my sneakers in the sink.

"What – are – you – doing?" she says.

"Getting banana, rotten banana, out of my sneakers."

Rachel's eyes narrow for a second. With her foaming mouth and wild bed hair Rachel looks rabid. "That bitch," she says.

The bus pumps diesel clouds into Jogja's polluted sky. Kransky stands by the door stretching her quads. She looks so healthy it makes me sick. Ibu Sujati stands next to her in a pink sweat suit and gold sun visor. Somehow I don't think she'll break a sweat today.

We drag ourselves up the steps to the bus. I'm cursing the teachers. After our breakthrough Michael and I had plans to shortlist possible schools for Devi, but now that has to wait. People are getting in my way. Again.

Libby's presence looms in the back row. She wants me to crack. Three strikes. It's not going to happen, but every squelchy step I take forces me to admit it might.

Our bus stops at a hillside village. We rub our eyes and stare at the idyllic patch of countryside with its gentle hills, curving stream and terraced rice paddy fields.

"This is so pretty," I say.

"Yeah, but that's not so scenic." Rachel tilts her head toward a group of older men dressed in running gear. Many of them have thick three-day growths and look hungover.

"Girls, come here!" Kransky waves us over. We trudge across the muddy ground and she introduces us to Alf, the Hash leader. He turns to greet us and a grin sweeps across his tanned face.

"Now, the trail today is easy to follow, but keep an eye out for signs. They could be chalk, flour, paper, or anything else I've managed to lay my hands on. If all else fails follow everyone else." He scratches his head. "There's a celebration at the end involving a lot of beer, but something tells me you won't be taking part in that."

We all snicker, except for Kransky.

"So, good luck, have fun, and Hash on," he says.

Rachel squashes a mosquito against her neck. I wiggle my toes, which are still damp, and wipe away the fog from the inside of my sunglasses.

Great, we haven't started and I'm already sweating buckets.

Alf blows a whistle and we're off. We surge forward in a sea of clammy flesh through shin-high grass. Cross-country running in this humidity is crazy. If Kransky wants us to experience expat culture, why couldn't we go to some over-the-top luxury day spa?

The older guys lead the pack. A couple of Chis girls bob along behind them. One of them looks like Marnie, Libby's minion.

"Can you see the evil one?" I strain to spot her in the pack.

"Nope," Rachel says. "Which is either a good thing or a Very Bad Thing."

After half an hour of crossing streams, leaping over logs, and weaving our way through rice paddies, my skin itches with grit, heat, and sweat. My feet are sore and my shoes are waterlogged. The sun beats down on us and the air smells of overripe fruit and damp grass. After a series of hills the pack has thinned out and the landscape has changed from rice paddies to jungles of bamboo and vines. We can't see the leaders or hear the cries of *on, on, on* anymore. We turn a corner and stop short. The path breaks into several directions and there's no one to follow.

We look at each other and shrug.

"Hey, what about that?" Rachel points to a stick of bamboo, partly camouflaged by a fallen branch, which is holding up a scrap of paper with an arrow on it. The arrow points toward the middle path.

"Looks a bit random but there's nothing else."

We take the middle path and continue running for another five minutes but there's no one ahead or behind us.

"Does this feel kind of wrong to you?" Rachel says.

"It's creepy quiet. It's never quiet here."

Rachel points to a chalk arrow on the side of a tree.

We keep jogging. A couple of minutes later we approach a group of farms made up of falling-down dwellings, with skinny chickens running about. Three kids squat in the dust playing marbles. They look up at us, then down at our sneakers and smile. We must look trashed. One of them whispers "*bules*" to the others, the Indonesian word for white people, and they giggle, but stop when they catch Rachel glaring at them.

"Rache, they're just kids."

"Yeah, I'm just annoyed."

"Me too."

There's a dirt path bordering a fence made of loosely-bound sticks. A cardboard arrow hangs from the fence.

"Let's go that way," I say, and we head toward it. The chickens stalk us.

A teenage boy emerges and wheels out a rickety bicycle from one of the shacks. "Not that way, the other path." He points in the opposite direction.

"Huh?" I look around but I can't see what he's talking about.

"But the sign points this way." Rachel frowns.

The boy jogs over to us.

"See that barn over there?" He points to a wooden structure behind a tree. "They all ran down that path."

"But there's no sign," Rachel says.

He swings around to the kids and asks them questions in rapid-fire dialect for a few seconds. We watch the to and fro between them. The chickens peck at the ground around our feet. Two of the kids shrug, but the eldest, a girl, answers him.

"She says the sign was on the tree before but someone moved it." He shakes his head.

"Did she see what this person looked like?" Rachel puts her hands on her hips.

The guy fires more questions at the child. "A girl . . . about your age. Blonde hair, this long." He holds his hand past his shoulder.

My nostrils flare. If I wasn't so furious, I'd be impressed.

With help from the neighbors, we find the best short cuts to take to rejoin the Hash. For half an hour we run down hills so steep we grab at branches and vines to break our fall. My banana-reeking sneakers have attracted a couple of jungle insects and we've collected some grotesque bites. We catch the tail of the Hash when we spy the last of the walkers.

"Hi girls," says a seventy-something woman with silver white hair. "What are you doing back here with us old farts?"

"Maggie!" Her companion shakes her head under her yellow cap.

"Don't ask," Rachel says. "Someone set us off course."

"Oh dear, I heard about a mix-up, but it was fixed by the time we reached it. Go down that hill and you'll be at the finish line before you know it."

We thank her and sprint downhill.

"Please let this be the end," I say.

"Please let me get hold of Libby." Rachel makes a strangling gesture with her hands.

But we round a corner and the valley rises to another steep peak.

"Fuck." Rachel stamps her foot in the dust.

After a grinding climb to the top, we nearly cry. The end of the Hash is at the bottom of the hill. We tear through the last fifty gravity-assisted yards, sick of the grit in our shoes, the sweat and dirt on our skins, the throb of insect bites, and the monumental snakiness of Libby Hartnett. Chis girls stop mid-conversation to watch our descent.

"Thank God. Here they are." Kransky rushes up to us. "I was planning a search party. What happened? You look a mess."

Libby stands to one side with Marnie. She watches us, gulping from a can of Coke Zero.

"Get lost." Rachel glares at Libby.

"What did you say?" Kransky steps closer to us.

"It's not worth it. Don't do it." I touch Rachel's arm.

"I could kill her," she says under her breath. She turns to Kransky. "We got lost. There was a mix-up with the signs. But some locals helped us get back on track."

Libby's hand is over her mouth, her shoulders shaking with laughter.

Kransky studies us. "We were so worried. As long as you're alright?"

We nod but we're scratching like fiends.

"What on earth has attacked you?" Kransky holds up Rachel's arm, which, like mine, is covered with mini, angry volcanoes.

I tear at my skin. The other Chis girls look relaxed. My eyes sting and I look up at the sky. Why can't I be tougher? A part of me wants to scratch Libby's eyes out, but another part of me, the six-year-old me, wants to yell, *Why are you so mean?*

Why does she get to me so much?

I scratch harder.

A barrel-shaped man waltzes up to us with a huge tankard of beer in his hand. He wears a white, beer-drenched T-shirt which is plastered to him and exaggerates the wobble of his belly. His sandy hair curls over the edges of a blue and white terry-toweling headband, making him look like a sweaty Roman emperor. He puffs on a cigarette stuck in the corner of his mouth and stares at my arm.

"Oh my, looks like one of the finest examples of Java jungle pox I've ever seen. Hold this please." The man deposits the tankard into Kransky's hands. He pulls the cigarette from his mouth, taps it so that flakes of white ash collect in his palm, and rubs the ash into one of my bites.

"Hey—" I say, but he shushes me, lights another cigarette, and continues rubbing ash into my other bites.

"How's it feel now?" He fixes his pale blue eyes on me.

"Better. Thanks." I inspect my arm.

"Never fails. Other arm." He taps out some more ash.

Rachel passes me a can of Fanta, condensation dripping from her fingers, and the man takes hold of her arm. I gulp Fanta and within seconds the syrupy orange goodness lifts me. Under his healing powers, the heat fades from Rachel's cheeks. She almost lost it with Libby before, but I want to hug her – she was protecting me, stopping me from lashing out and earning my third strike.

Libby is alone now, slumped against a tree, her eyes downcast. It's a look I recognize from another time, but I can't place when. Stokes' words come back to me: *Most bullies are acting out their own pain. It's about them. Don't let her drag you under*. She'd sabotaged the Hash, snitched on me after Merapi, and been a giant pain in the ass, but she hadn't won. I'd kept it together.

While Rache showers my mind is in hyperdrive. We know Devi's school is close to the Pineapple Village and a bus ride away from Salatiga. Like they say on crime shows, we can *triangulate the location.* We just don't have the holographic programs they play with.

I search for high schools near Salatiga and find too many to deal with. The information online is patchy, but I dig deeper and eliminate junior high schools and end up with a list of five high schools. Then I strike out a boys' school and a Christian one. I roll over on the bed and message Michael: *Down to 3 schools! Once we check the bus routes we'll find it.*

Michael messages straight back: *I'll check the buses. Send the list.*

I'm back in the café working through the mountain of homework Sutopo gave me in our last class. I'm itching to find Devi's school, so I bargain with myself. An hour of homework buys half an hour of research. Citra seems to be doing something similar, except with cigarettes.

There's nothing from Michael yet.

Turn the page, find the next question. Keep going.

After forty-five minutes I've finished a section and a small mosquito is dive-bombing my ear. Arief told me that the daytime ones carry dengue fever. It zeroes in on me and I swat it but it slips away. On Google I research bus routes to Salatiga but it's a mess – there are timetables but there's hardly any route information.

Citra scrapes her chair back and walks outside.

"What's the problem?" Arief wanders over from behind the counter. "You have no coffee?"

"I wish it was that."

"Maybe I can help?"

I meet his curious eyes. "I'm trying to find buses to Salatiga." I explain the locations of the schools.

"OK. Not this. Useless." He points to my phone. "Wait." He sails back through the kitchen doors and reappears with a map with the bus routes marked. "See, much better." He traces the routes to Salatiga with his finger.

"Do they go to Pineapple Village?"

He frowns and examines the map. "Only this bus."

"What about these schools?" I show him the list on my phone.

"This route goes past this school, another goes to this one and another to the last school."

"What do you mean?"

"Three buses, each one goes to Salatiga and to one of these schools." He smiles.

"Three different lines?" So much for hoping this

would narrow the schools down.

Arief's smile droops.

"Thanks Arief," I say quickly. "You're a massive help."

He lets me borrow the map and darts over to a new customer. I glare at the three red dots on the map and let out the groan I've been holding in.

Michael: *Sorry. Family thing went all night. In my honor so no escape. Can u get away?*

Me: *Can't. Sorry.*

Michael: *That sucks. Yandra isn't working and we could check out those schools today.*

Me: *But it's Sunday! Not open.*

Michael: *Crap. Will see when he can do it.*

We've got two days left to find Devi's school and Yuliana. *Two days.* Don't you get it, Michael?

On Monday when the bus dumps me back at the hotel I race to the café. Citra greets me and Michael's already there. My shoulders unknot at the sight of him. I make a big display out of getting my homework out and sit on the same side of the table as him. Citra can only see the backs of our heads.

"Where have you been?" I whisper out of the side of my mouth.

"Sorry. The reception's rubbish at my auntie's and she kind of kidnapped me—"

"Really?"

"Sometimes she smothers me. She feels guilty . . ."

"Why?"

"It's because of Mum. She feels bad for us." He rushes through his words and his eyes skitter away.

Citra sighs loudly. She stretches her arms high and arches her back. Arief gazes after her as she strides outside. He grabs a bowl of peanuts and follows her.

"What happened to your mum?"

He pulls back from the table and his eyes seem to darken. "Ovarian cancer. Four years ago."

"That must have been . . ." My throat tightens and I run out of words.

He stares at the table. "It blew our world apart. But the worst part wasn't her death, it was the dying. Before Mum was like this force, but it destroyed her from the inside." He pushes his palms against his thighs.

"I'm so sorry. I shouldn't have asked."

He finally meets my eyes. "No, it's good. I've got friends I've known for years and anytime it comes up, or gets close to it, they do the big swerve."

I clutch my hands together under the table.

"They're just uncomfortable," he goes on. "Sometimes

I want to talk about Mum but it's hard to bring it up, a bit of a downer, you know, so it's good you came straight out and asked."

"If you want to talk about her, I'm here."

"Thanks. But not right now." He gives me a smile that's playful and sad and it makes my heart ache in a big way. "Hey, you free tomorrow? Yandra can take us."

My heart soars. "Tomorrow's great because they're on an all-day excursion to Prambanan. They don't get back until five."

"That gives us heaps of time. Yandra reckons it will take us over two hours to get to the first school and we can do a loop of them in an hour. But what about Citra?"

"Think I'll have a monster case of gastro."

He smiles. "I've got a good feeling about tomorrow."

"I keep thinking I imagined all this, despite everything. It's because it's in the pages of a diary and it's . . ." I wave my hand.

"Abstract?"

"Yeah." The feeling lifts when I'm around Michael. When I'm alone it wheels around and around, like a dog chasing its tail.

"At least we've got a plan," he says.

"Tomorrow's going to be epic."

Tonight we have our farewell dinner at a Padang restaurant with all the teachers from the language school. Waiters cover our two long tables with dish after dish of food. We pick only what we want – succulent beef rendang, fish curry, satay – and leave the tripe and intestines for dead.

When I bite into the chili eggplant the flesh is soft and slides down my throat. The chili makes the sides of my tongue curl. The taste transports me to Oma's house, where we used to eat small bowls of her rice and chili eggplant with our fingers.

"This is so good." Rache points with her spoon.

I eat another piece, but when I think of Devi the food sours and I push the bowl away.

We return to the hotel and I say my goodnights. I'm ready to bolt upstairs, burrow under my quilt and stew in the injustice of it all, when Ibu Sujati pulls me aside. Her hand rests on my forearm, orange-red nail polish bright against my arm.

"Melati, Pak Sutopo told me how hard you've worked. You've made great progress."

"Thanks." I glance toward the stairs.

"Tomorrow we have a special trip to Prambanan and since you've worked so hard, we've decided you'll be joining us." She pats my arm.

No. No. No.

"Are you alright, Mel?" Her bright eyes sweep over me.

"Thanks. Sounds good." My voice is flat.

"Are you sure you're alright?"

I fake a smile. "I'm OK. How exciting."

"See you in the morning then."

I nod. When she turns away I swear under my breath.

TWENTY-ONE

When my alarm wakes me at 6.15, Rache doesn't stir. I turn up the A/C and message Ibu Sujati: *Ibu, been up all night with food poisoning. Too sick to go to the temples. Need to stay in bed and sleep. Really* ☹ *to miss out.*

At six-thirty my phone rings.

"Hello?" I croak.

"You sound awful. Are you OK?" Ibu Sujati says.

"Not really." I shiver.

Nails tap on something hard. "Maybe I should check on you?"

"It's OK. I've got gastrolyte and aspirin. I just need to sleep and . . . be close to a toilet."

"What a shame. I thought you looked a bit funny last night."

"Must have been getting sick." My teeth chatter, the A/C is really kicking in.

"We'll be back at five. I would stay but we need two

staff to escort the girls. I'll get the hotel staff to check on you."

My heart pounds. "That's OK. I'm going to put the 'do not disturb' sign on the door and sleep."

"Are you sure?"

"Yeah, can't believe I'll miss the temples though." I want to vomit in my mouth, but I have to be convincing.

"I'll check on you when we return. Take care."

Michael: *They've gone.*

Me: *Be down in two.*

I stuff spare clothes under my sheets, mould them into a Mel shape and pull a sheet over the lump's head. It's crappy but there's no time. I grab my daypack. The "do not disturb" sign swings from the door knob when I lock it behind me.

In stealth mode, I run downstairs. At the bottom I hang off the last step and peek around the corner. No one is around. I duck past the counter, out the front door, past two new arrivals who look like Scandinavian goddesses. They've mesmerized the staff. I dart past unnoticed and rush next door where Michael is waiting.

"Hey, made it." I run up to him.

"Did anyone see you?" Michael says.

"Don't think so. Where's Yandra?"

Michael runs his fingers through his hair. "He got called into work."

My breath catches. "So we can't –"

He holds up a hand. "I hired one. It's just up the street."

I grin. "Awesome!"

"No problem. I want to find her too."

My smile lingers until we break eye contact.

We pick up the scooter from a shop up the street, in the thick of the backpacker zone.

"Hop on."

"Do you know how to drive one of these?"

"Yeah, I've been riding them for years." He grins. "Trust me."

What choice do I have? We have to find Yuliana today.

Michael holds out a helmet.

"Where's yours?" I frown.

"They only gave us one. No spares."

"No, you have it." I pass it back to him but he pushes it away. I can't help but feel guilty when I slide the helmet on.

Michael jumps on first and I sit behind him. We're a squishy fit, but I've seen five people on bikes smaller than this. The scooter splutters, then Michael takes off, ripping up dust behind him. We gun it down our street, dodging *becaks*, their drivers pumping hard on the pedals, old women hauling baskets of vegetables, and a truck loaded with wood. We weave down tight lanes where Michael beeps at chickens straggling across our path and children yell *Hello mister* at us.

We make a wide hard turn on to the highway. He guns it and the scooter sputters and chokes for a second before it recovers. This hairdryer on wheels can't keep up with the utes and trucks beside us, but we pass a horse dragging a carriage, its muscles shining with sweat.

I grip Michael, his waist warm under my hands. I turn my head to watch the traffic and swallow a mouthful of fumes from a rusty truck. I swing my head the other way and watch as palm trees appear. The sun's on my back and a grin spreads across my face. After all the waiting and wangling and lying we're on our way, getting closer to Devi every second.

Michael slows and turns into a muddy parking area on the side of the road. He parks next to a guy with bottles of soft drink perched on top of two crates. The soft drink looks odd, a chemical yellow color, not the usual orange or cola colors. Michael pays him and we hop off the bike and stretch. The seller pulls the seat up, unscrews the nozzle on the gas tank beneath the seat and pours a full bottle into the tank.

I laugh. "I really thought that was soft drink."

Michael smiles. "Yeah, the first time I saw it I told Yandra it would ruin his engine."

I stretch my quads. "My butt is killing me."

Michael glances at my butt and then looks away. I turn away and smirk. He fumbles in the pocket of his cargos, fishes out his inhaler and sucks on it.

"My lungs feel like crap." He inhales again, his face pale. "It's like sucking on an exhaust out there."

"You OK?"

"Just a bit tight." He presses his hand to his chest.

I pass the helmet to him. "Take it, might stop you sucking down so much."

"It's fine."

Michael walks up to one of the neighboring stalls and grabs handfuls of snacks I've never seen before. He opens a packet of peanuts coated in a spicy shell and we demolish them in minutes.

"I'm doing well for someone with gastro." I make a face.

"Must be a great actor." He smirks.

"When I'm motivated."

"We'll need our best acting today at those high schools." Michael wipes his hand over his mouth and passes the remaining snacks to me. I stuff them into my backpack.

There's no feeling in my bum and my thighs are numb. We're almost moulded together on the bike. A few times the vibration of the bike and the fumes have made my eyelids droop and I've woken seconds later with my helmet bashing Michael's back.

The highway stretches on. The same cars, swarms of bikes, dodgy-looking trucks and vans pumping out fumes, but the rows of palm trees are thicker here, and there are random glimpses of jungle and village.

He turns on to a minor road and within minutes we're puttering through a village of brick houses and simple shacks. Michael twists around, the sunlight reflecting off his aviator glasses. "The school's minutes away."

Adrenaline swamps my veins. We fly over a deep pothole and I slam into Michael.

"Sorry." He looks over his shoulder.

"Watch out!" I grip his waist.

There are more potholes than road. He steers around them and the road evens out. We breeze past a bamboo shack where a bunch of workers are resting in the shade. On a large pitch teenagers in blue and white uniforms are playing soccer and there's a pale green weathered building at the end of the field.

"Is that it?" My voice is thin.

"Must be."

We park and I clamber off. My pants look wrecked. I try to dust them off but manage to rub the dirt deeper into the fabric. Great first impression I'll make. My hair must look feral after spending so long on the bike.

"Ready?" Michael says.

I force a smile.

We follow the signs for reception down a long, covered walkway. A high-pitched bell rings and students flow from the classrooms. We're surrounded by blue and white uniforms, boys and girls, their voices rising, staring and smiling at us. We try to pass but we're stuck. Two girls on my right gaze at me, whispering to each other.

"Where are … you from?" the closest girl says in halting English.

"Australia," I say.

She nods. "Very nice."

They look about sixteen, Devi's age.

"Does Ibu Yuliana teach here?" I ask.

The girl beside me nods. "Oh, Ibu Yuliana. She is good."

My heart takes a running leap. I thank them and they enter a classroom yards away.

I grab Michael's arm. "She's here."

He grins back at me.

We reach reception and a frail man is standing at the desk, propping himself up on the counter and leafing through a bunch of forms. The perky young guy behind the counter takes a form from the top of thc pile and gives the man instructions. The old man grips a pen, his hand shaking as he fills out entries.

I roll my eyes at Michael. This is going to take forever.

The receptionist tells us to take a seat while we wait. We flop onto a wooden bench and I check the time on my phone. Ten-thirty.

Eight minutes later the receptionist calls us over and we ask for Ibu Yuliana.

"Do you have an appointment?" His eyes flicker over us.

We shake our heads. He checks something on his computer. "Her class finishes in twenty minutes. She may have a few minutes to meet you."

I watch the clock behind reception and chew on a fingernail. In seconds I've ripped it down to the pink flesh. I pull my hands on to my lap. Michael is tapping his foot and he passes an earbud to me. The music is melodic, electronic and soothing. I hum along to it.

We jump when the bell rings. The receptionist picks up the phone, nods at us and minutes later a woman in her late thirties in a yellow lace jacket and white hijab walks up, giving us a wide, kind smile.

"I'm Yuliana. You wanted to speak to me?" she says in American-accented English.

We jump up. "Yes, I'm Mel and this is Michael."

"What is this about?"

"We found a student's diary and we're trying to return it to her. We're not sure if she goes to this school, but she might be in your class because she mentions an Ibu Yuliana." My voice cracks and I pull the diary out of my daypack.

She squints at us. "What's her name?"

"Devi. We don't know her surname."

"I have a Devi Iskurniawati in one of my classes."

"Really?"

"How old is she, Ibu?" Michael says.

"Nearly eighteen."

"Oh." My shoulders sag. "This Devi turned sixteen in January."

"You don't teach anyone else called Devi?" Michael says.

"No." She checks her watch. "Is there anything else I can help you with?"

We shake our heads and thank her.

Damn, damn, damn.

The last school is crumbling but pretty. It must have been painted lemon yellow years ago because now there are mouldy and bare patches in the paintwork. With its terracotta roof and wooden shutters it's charming. We ride up to the car park and my pulse beats in my ears.

The second school was a dead end with no teachers named Yuliana, so this is it.

Our last chance.

When I pull off my helmet I can't hear my pulse anymore but my heart is tripping. At reception we ask a young woman in a hijab for Ibu Yuliana. She asks us for our ID. We show her our passports and she takes them, then disappears into an office. She returns with photocopies of our passports.

"What's your business with Ibu Yuliana?"

"We found something that belongs to ... her and want to return it."

"You can leave it here, I'll give it to her." The woman raises her chin.

"But—" I start.

"Sorry Ibu, but it's important that we give it to her personally. Please?" Michael dips his head and smiles, looking up at her through his lashes.

I almost laugh.

After a long moment she picks up the phone and speaks to someone. "She's in class. Please wait." She waves us to some wooden chairs against the wall.

Michael and I pace the narrow corridor, our shoes

slapping the vinyl floor. I stare at the rows of photos on the wall. A school choir, all bright faces, shiny hair, and wide smiles. A school play. Trophy winners from a Math Olympiad. Boys' and girls' soccer teams. Devi never mentioned anything but singing and drawing. I study the choir photo, the hopeful faces. Are you in there, Devi?

"What's the time?" I say.

Michael points to the clock on the opposite wall.

It's 12.45. We've been waiting five minutes. Killer.

A bell sounds, doors swing open, and bodies pelt down the corridor. Michael's expression is trance-like as he stares at his phone. Two teachers walk down the corridor and when they speak to the receptionist my heart hitches for a second. But they walk on.

"Hello?" An elegant woman in her forties with her hair coiled low at the back of her head approaches. Her long, fitted batik skirt rustles as she glides toward us. "You were looking for me? I'm Ibu Yuliana."

"I'm Mel and this is Michael."

Her hand is cool and smooth when I shake it. Michael leaps up. She looks from me to Michael, and back again.

Words catch in my throat. "We're here about a student. Do you teach a girl named Devi?"

Her face lightens. “Yes,” she says, “but she went away.”

My heart freefalls. I show her the diary and she reaches for it.

“I gave that to her last year.” Her eyes flash. “Where did you find it?”

“In Melbourne, in Australia.”

“She’s a nanny there.” Yuliana opens the diary, scans a page.

Michael and I exchange glances and he nods.

I spit out the words. “We think she’s in trouble.”

TWENTY-TWO

We're in an office with arctic air-conditioning and the diary is in the middle of the table, cover facing up. Yuliana reaches for it again and flicks through it, studies the drawings.

"That's her handwriting. Her drawings. She's so talented, so artistic."

Something blooms in my chest. Is it relief that we've found Yuliana? That this is real? But then the feeling hardens as I realize what this means.

"I never wanted her to go. It never felt right. What's happened to her?" Yuliana turns another page.

"She's not a nanny. We've been translating this and we think she's been tricked." My eyes meet Michael's and he nods. "They're forcing her to work in a brothel."

She closes the diary slowly. "Could it be a mistake?"

"I got the same translation," Michael says.

"It does happen. I've heard of it. But I've never had a student . . ." She trails off.

"Do you know an Ibu Sri? Devi talked about Ibu Sri lining up the job, someone her dad knew."

She shakes her head. "Her family were really struggling. Brokers sometimes approach desperate families and offer them loans for their child's labor. The child has to work off the debt, but sometimes they trick them into other work. Do you know where she is?"

"We know she's in Melbourne and she gives a bit of a description of the brothel but not much," Michael says.

"That's why we searched for you. All we had was her name," I say.

"I haven't heard from Devi since she left." She clasps her hands together in her lap. "It's not like her, she should have been in touch."

"Have you seen her parents since she left?" Michael says.

"Not yet. I'll see if they've heard anything from her. Maybe they're already looking for her but want to keep it quiet. Devi's parents are very kind people, very traditional. This would . . ." She clears her throat. "I'll see if they've gone to the police."

The police. Of course, if Devi's parents haven't heard from her they might have talked to the police already.

"I go back to Melbourne tomorrow. Have you got a photo of Devi?"

Yuliana nods, her eyes watery. "I'll take care of this. If I find out anything I'll let you know." She writes her details on a piece of paper and passes it to me.

She flips through the book again and it falls open on the page I've struggled with most. When she flinches I know what she's reading; I saw the same look on Pak Sutopo's face.

"*Ayam potong.*" She gulps.

"What does that mean, Ibu?"

"It's a term for a new prostitute, one who has been cut off from her family."

After Ibu Yuliana photocopies the diary, she walks us back to the scooter. At the bottom of the stairs she stops and clutches the copy to her chest. "Thank you for bringing this to me. She's very clever finding a way to get this out. I'll make sure the police know and do everything I can. Promise me you'll stop investigating this. It's too dangerous. Leave it with me."

I hesitate, but her eyes are determined. She's not going to forget Devi. "We will," I say.

She nods. "Safe travels."

I slide my helmet on and Michael starts the engine.

He yells goodbye over the engine noise. We wave and take off. Over my shoulder I see Yuliana watching us, her face fierce.

I prise Devi's photo out of my pocket and study it. Devi's a real girl, she's not some ghost in a diary. This is her school, this is her teacher, and those girls walking by in uniforms could be her friends. It's not the best shot, it's taken from a group photo, but Devi's wide smile and girlish ponytail hurt me all the same. I pull my visor down, and start to cry.

TWENTY-THREE

We've been on the highway for half an hour when the scooter moans. Michael turns his head and says something I don't catch. About half a mile later the scooter groans and sputters, like it's losing power. Michael steers to the side of the road where there's a strip of dirt between the highway and a deep water-filled ditch. I slide off the bike, nearly falling into the ditch. Michael can't get the engine to turn over. He jumps off, frowns and checks all the gauges.

I kick myself for calling it a hairdryer on wheels. Maybe I've jinxed it.

"What's wrong?"

"No idea. I don't know anything about mechanical stuff."

"Yeah, same. Did the hire place give you a number to ring?"

"Let me try again first." He hops back on and tries to start it up, but it won't catch. It's dead. "Crap." He kicks the tire then takes out his phone. He mashes the phone against his ear and turns his back to me, trying to hear over the buzz of traffic.

It's 2.55. We'll still make it if we can get the scooter moving.

There's a steady river of traffic on the highway, pumping out nasty fumes. I perch against the scooter and think about Ibu Yuliana. No wonder Devi admires her, she's such an elegant, sophisticated woman. Her English is amazing and she cares so much about Devi. I could definitely have a crush on her.

Teacher crushes.

Eek.

Michael's face is screwed up. "They said they could come and pick us up."

"Great."

"In three hours."

I frown at him. "Why so long?"

"No spare cars."

I look up at the sky and punch my fists at the air. "Why are you doing this to me?"

Michael snorts.

"I am in so much shit." How stupid was I to think I could fake being sick, sneak out, find Devi's teacher and get back in time for dinner? Why don't I ever think beyond the first rush of an idea?

After twenty or so demon buses have blasted us, and Michael has sucked on his inhaler for the tenth time, and he's tried and failed to start the scooter for the millionth time, I stick out my thumb at passing trucks. After a couple of minutes a truck with an open tray at the back, loaded with bulging hessian sacks, lurches to a stop beside us, almost barreling us into the ditch.

"Woah!" We dodge out of the way.

"Where you going?" a young skinny guy in a Manchester United T-shirt yells through the open window.

"Jogjakarta," Michael says.

The guy next to the driver wakes up. He hangs over the window, his rockabilly quiff tumbling forward, and points to our bike.

"Stuffed," Michael says.

"Hmmm." Rockabilly leaps down from the truck, inspects the scooter and turns the key like Michael has already done a hundred times. The driver joins him and they hold the scooter up by the handlebars and shake it.

"Should they be doing that?" I whisper.

"Probably not." Michael frowns.

They lower the bike down and Rockabilly slaps the seat. "*Rusak*."

Rusak, broken, is now my most hated Indonesian word.

"We give you lift? Put it in the back." The driver tilts his head toward the tray.

We hoist the scooter up and Rockabilly shoves some of the bags full of firewood out of the way to make room. He holds out his hand and helps me and Michael up.

Rockabilly prods one of the sacks with the toe of his black cowboy boot. "Wake up." He snorts when the rumpled head of a guy in an AC/DC T-shirt pops up, his eyes half-closed. AC/DC swings a fist at Rockabilly's legs.

"We have new friends. Make room," Rockabilly says.

AC/DC blinks at us and smiles. He pushes some of the bags out of the way. The truck takes off and I fall back against a sack and firewood jabs my butt. The hard metal surface of the tray has a griddle pattern; by the time we reach Jogja my bum's going to look like a waffle. But we'll make it by 4.30.

Easy.

AC/DC strums a guitar and the music's nothing like his T-shirt, it's gentle and flowing. His long skinny fingers work the strings like he's speaking a language. Michael takes over and plays "Highway to Hell." I laugh and our eyes meet, his eyes smiling, and something lifts in my chest and floats there for a second.

The truck squeals to a stop and catapults me forward. I open my eyes and AC/DC and Michael are hanging over the left side of the tray, talking to Rockabilly.

"What's going on?" I crawl forward.

"We're out of fuel." Michael tugs his hands through his hair.

"How the hell did that happen?"

"Faulty fuel gauge apparently. And the nearest gas station isn't close."

I check the time on my phone: almost 4.30. We should've been back by now. It's built up here, with houses studding the surrounding hills, and the highway's more congested.

"How far's Jogja?"

"About nine miles," Michael says.

I could hitch the rest of the way, but that wouldn't be fair on Michael. He'd be left to deal with the scooter when he'd hired it to help me. And since when did hitching enter the realm of Things I Do?

Rockabilly's on the phone, drawling his words with no sign of panic.

"What are they doing? We have to go."

Michael gives me a sympathetic look. "They're doing us a favor."

He's right, but he's not the one with expulsion hanging over him.

AC/DC walks to the side of the truck, removes the fuel cap and holds it out so passing drivers will see we've run out.

Clever.

No one stops. Despite all the fumes, AC/DC looks like he's made of marble. About seventy yards away there's a teenage boy on a motorbike with a crate of soft drink bottles on the back. I wave at him like I'm possessed and he finally notices. He weaves through the traffic and pulls up beside us. AC/DC high fives him.

Disaster averted.

We're cruising down the highway with a full tank. It's 4.44 pm.

"What is wrong?" AC/DC says.

"If I'm not back by five I'll be expelled." A little speed racer has taken up residence in my heart.

"School? They teach nothing about life."

"True. But if I get expelled my parents are going to send me to this fascist school. In the country. I won't have a life."

"Is problem." He crouches, twists over the side of the truck and shouts something to Rockabilly. Then he slides back into the tray. "Don't worry. Five o'clock, all good."

Through the rear window I watch Rockabilly talk to the driver. The truck revs so hard we're all flung backward.

AC/DC can't stop giggling. "Sigit likes to race."

The truck hoons and slices past other vehicles. I shut my eyes as we cut past a family of five on a motorbike, missing them by inches. I grip the side of the tray.

"Fun ride!" Michael yells.

I grimace.

Within minutes the highway ends and we plunge into the streets of Jogja. The truck slows down because there's not enough room to dodge the peak-hour traffic, random oldies and schoolkids. I wrap my arms around my knees. We have to make it.

Sigit yells out the window at us. I snap to attention. We're at the far end of my street.

"Yes, but up the other end." My heart pumps.

Sigit salutes with his hand and turns back to the road.

It's 4.53. I grin at Michael and AC/DC. "I might make it."

"I told you no problem," AC/DC says.

Michael scoots next to me, his knee brushing mine. "When we get there, you jump out, I'll deal with the bike, OK?"

"Thanks. You're the best."

His face softens and he shifts back next to AC/DC. He looks over the side of the truck, but I can't bring myself to.

"Ah, Mel," Michael says, his body still over the side of the truck.

"Yeah?"

"I can see the bus."

I squeeze in next to him. The yellow bus is about to pull up at the hotel. This can't be happening.

"Shit. There's no way I can get into the hotel without them seeing."

"There's a way." Michael grabs my hand.

AC/DC tells Sigit to stop.

"Can you wait? I'll come back for the scooter," Michael says.

"No problem," Sigit says.

"Thank you, thank you so much. For everything," I say to them. Rockabilly gives us a thumbs up.

AC/DC opens the tray for us and we scramble to the ground. Michael tugs my arm and we crouch and peek around the truck, but no one's left the Chis bus yet. Still crouching, we dart across the street, sprint up a lane by the side of a bookshop. We burn up it, dodging schoolkids and shoppers. A schoolbag slams into my thigh but I ignore the jab of pain and sprint for my life. At the end we turn left into a narrower lane.

"This way," Michael says, panting.

Baskets of rubbish and empty tins of palm oil are

stacked at the back of a string of restaurants. We reach a cracked brick wall topped with terracotta tiles and creepers.

"This is it." Michael stops.

I swallow. The wall is about two yards high. "How am I going to get over that?"

"Same way I did the other night, but I'll give you a boost."

"You did this?"

"Yeah, you need a key for the front door when it's late."

I glance at the top.

"It's better than it looks. There's a soft grass patch to land on."

If I don't jump I'll be sprung in minutes. The teachers will waste no time checking on me.

Michael bends, cups his hands together and I step into his hold and grab at the wall, scratching for handholds in the cracks. I try to drag myself up to the terracotta tiles but I'm falling. He pushes my feet but I still can't quite reach.

"Boost me up!"

Michael hesitates.

"Come on!" I yell.

He shoves me up by my butt. I grip the top of the

wall, pull myself up and swing my legs over, yelling, "See ya" as I drop over the wall.

The ground is spongy when I land, but pain shoots from my ankles to my shins. Through the gardens I hear Australian accents – Chis girls – coming closer. I run past the wall of bamboo and palms, and up the stairs, battling my screaming shins. I fumble with my key and open the door just in time. Door closed, I hear Chis girls walking by. Panting, I strip off my clothes, pull on an oversized T-shirt and shorts, and jump into bed.

Chest heaving, I wait for the knock to come.

It's our last night in Indonesia and Rache and I can't bear to leave without a final *martabak manis*. She's still bloated from dinner and I'm pretending to be delicate after my day of throwing up, so we share a pancake. We sit by the side of the road near *martabak manis* man's cart, with taxi and rickshaw drivers, students, and a heavily pregnant woman. Cigarette smoke drifts toward me, but after this long in Indonesia I don't bother to wave it away. Last time I was here Libby was sneaking a smoke across the street and I was bracing for a showdown. Now she feels more distant than ever, but I can't let my guard down.

"I've definitely put on weight here." Rachel releases

the top button of her jeans. She looks at my waist. "But you look the same. It's not fair."

My mouth is gummed up with chocolate and condensed milk. I have to chew and chew and chew before I can speak. "I've sweated so much it kind of balanced out."

Tomorrow we'll fly home and my parents are not going to be happy. There could be a shitstorm at school but I'll deal with it. For now I relish the buttery sweetness in my mouth. I wriggle on the footpath and think of my birthmark. I can't always be good, but at least I'm not a big fat fake anymore.

"What's been your favorite bit of this trip?" Rachel says.

"That's hard. There's so much."

"It's easy for me. Just being here. All of this." She spreads her arms. "Soaking it up."

"Yeah, you're right. It's everything."

It's lava spray. The smell of satay at night. Diving deep with my Indonesian. Meeting Michael. Arief looking out for me. An Indonesian punk band. Birds of paradise and ginger plants. Little kids waving at us. The kindness of three cool guys in a truck.

We love the same things about Indonesia, but we've been on two different trips. She'd kill me if she knew how I'd barely made it over the wall.

Today Yuliana stepped out of the diary and into our lives. It's real now. I'm on the edge of something and I'm dizzy, wondering how the hell I'm going to find Devi.

TWENTY-FOUR

I wake to a Melbourne sunset and a dried drool noodle on my cheek. We disembark in silence and stand zombie-like in the immigration and customs queues. None of us want to admit that our adventure is over.

The automatic doors open at the arrivals area and Mum's behind the barrier rail. In her indigo smock top she stands out from the crowd. I yell out and push my cart toward her. She gives me a big squeeze and looks me up and down.

"You look like a drug mule. Are you sick?"

"I'm OK." That final *martabak manis* pushed my guts to the limit last night, but thanks to Mrs. OBB's poo-stoppers I survived the flight without embarrassment.

Chis girls hug their families or act cool after their sudden taste of independence. Mum takes my cart and charges toward the exit. I wave goodbye to Rache and mime phoning her.

“So, how was it?” Mum strides toward the car park.

“It was amazing. My Indonesian’s heaps better.” I trot after her.

“Glad you had a good time.”

I study her face; there’s no hint of sarcasm. But then in the car Mum’s lips press together into a sharp line. “Melati,” she starts, “when the school called, you’ve got no idea how much it stressed me.” Her jaw is steel as she merges into traffic.

I hold my breath.

“A volcano, a bloody volcano.” She shakes her head.

“I know it was stupid.” I shrink in my chair.

“Don’t you think? About the risks?”

“Sorry.”

“Don’t apologize, I need to get angry with you.”

I fold my arms across my chest.

“After everything that’s happened, that fight and the meditation thing.”

“*Mediation*.”

“What?”

“Mediation. It was a mediation. You said meditation.”

“Don’t you . . .” She shoots me a death glare, her nostrils flare and the car swerves.

“Watch the road.”

“You—”

A driver honks at her, gives her the finger and overtakes us.

"Yeah, what?" she shouts.

I grip the handlebar above the door.

"You could've been expelled," she says. "You know that, don't you?"

Thank God she doesn't know about me stealing the diary and my trip to find Ibu Yuliana.

"How could you be so reckless?"

I stare straight ahead at a Hello Kitty doll waving from the rear window of the hatchback in front of us.

"You've got nothing to say?" She shakes her head.

I keep staring at the road. Along the highway hundreds of headlights are reaching for Melbourne.

"And who's this boy they caught you with?"

I finally speak. "Michael."

"Michael?"

"Yep."

"For God's sake, that's all you've got to say?"

"Jeez, Mum, what do you want to know?"

She takes a deep breath, like Stokes has taught me to do in anger management. "I know testing limits is part of the deal, but a boy – that's all you need right now."

"You had a full-on boyfriend at my age—"

"But I wasn't bloody sneaking out to climb volcanoes

with him." Her hands clench the steering wheel. "And I wasn't on thin ice at school."

"Because you dropped out." If you do the math, Mum fell pregnant with Samuel in Year Twelve. Through my hair, I sneak a look at her. Her chin wobbles.

Crap. I feel like I've killed her puppy.

"He's a friend," I say.

"A friend?"

"Yeah. It's not like we're doing anything. We're not even kissing."

She drums her fingers on the steering wheel, a sure sign that she's dying for a cigarette.

"He's a cool guy. He's been helping me with my Indonesian. I know it was totally stupid of me to get caught—"

"Get caught? Get caught! That's what you think you did wrong? Not sneaking out, not risking death by toxic fumes, but getting caught."

It's all true. I'd do it all again, but I'd do a better job of avoiding Libby.

"You'll lose your scholarship if you keep going this way. It's your last chance. Don't blow it."

"I know. I know."

She takes our exit. "There's a warning letter from the scholarship committee waiting for you at home."

It's almost six when I wake with a shudder. Hedy, snoozing beside me, stiffens. It's the silence of our street – broken only by the occasional rattle of a tram – that has woken me. My ears are tuned to the constant noise of Indonesia and it's too quiet to sleep here.

I turn on my lamp, find Devi's photo in my bedside cabinet and study her. Her carefree smile and perfect ponytail, shoulder to shoulder with other smiling girls. Like she mentioned, she looks older than sixteen.

Where are you, Devi?

It's useless, we've got no way of tracking her down. I was an idiot to think I could deal with this, it's too much. Then I remember that in Jogja it seemed doomed when we didn't know how to find Ibu Yuliana. But we worked through it, and we can do it again. There's got to be something that will help us.

But we promised Yuliana we'd stop investigating. We just have to wait for her. I sink against my pillows and try to stop thinking about it. I scroll through crap on my phone for a while but it's hopeless – ideas and questions keep coming at me.

On a scrap of paper I write down what we know.

Melbourne

Blue glow (a blue light?)

Window painted over

Green vine

Silver tree (is she upstairs?)

Quiet street

Needle in a fricking haystack. I pin the clues up over my desk.

"What are you doing?" Mum sticks her head around my door. "I heard movement."

"Stuff." I swing around. "Guess I'm jetlagged."

Mum's already dressed in her massage gear. "You feeling OK?"

"Think so."

"What's that?" She steps toward me and points to the list of clues on the wall.

I wish I could tell her but ever since Year Nine it's like she's been looking for proof that I'm bad. All she would think about is the school expelling me for stealing the file. It would be *hello brat camp* before I could blink.

"Oh, it's for school," I say. "Creative writing exercise. For English. We've got to use all the words in a composition."

"Right." She nods. "Well, I've got an early start. Take it easy today. OK?" She squeezes my shoulder.

"Yeah." I watch the door close behind her and turn back to my list. When did I get so good at lying?

I glare at the list. *Blue glow*. Why would the building have a blue glow? Must be weird lighting or something.

A silver tree. What's with that? An artificial tree? On my phone I search for silver trees and find bad Christmas ones, spray-painted silver.

A brothel with a Christmas tree?

I pace around my room and send an email to Ibu Yuliana, asking if she has any news. Devi's parents must be going crazy worrying about her.

There's a Big Fat Nothing from Michael. Why does it annoy me? It's not like I *like* him. But the back of my throat feels tight when I think of him. I miss seeing him every day. We'd promised to meet up as soon as he flew back and work out what to do about Devi. So why hasn't he contacted me?

Screw it.

I grab my phone to call him but it's only 6.57. I tap my fingers against the screen. Normal people are asleep. I toss my phone back on to my bed.

My eyes wander back to the list. I'm missing something.

Kurt.

When I google combinations of *Kurt, brothel, escort, pimp, massage,* and *Melbourne* I end up with gross photos of an oiled male escort named Kurt, but no pimp.

Guess Kurt's not going to publish his CV online.

Why can't anything about this be easy? Every second we waste means more horror piles up on Devi. I kick my leg out against my desk and spin around in my chair.

But I promised Yuliana. I need to be patient and trust that she's all over it. On my phone I find footage of Lina, the wild singer in Jogja. I slide the volume to full blast and scream along with her.

"No offence, Mr. Stokes, but you look like sh –, er, stuffed," I say.

The chair groans when he sags back into it and folds one long leg on top of the other. He's wearing a cable knit sweater, worn khaki pants, and Birkenstocks. He looks like a fisherman, not a surfer, but I guess he has a fisherman's patience, listening to me and the other girls day after day, hoping for a bite.

Stokes gestures for me to sit. I sink into the armchair and stare up at him. Maybe he can help us find Devi? But what am I thinking – if he finds out I stole the file I'll end up in brat camp. Michael thinks Stokes must be dodgy but he's wrong.

Not. This. Guy.

There must be an explanation for how Devi's diary ended up in his office, a good one.

"I was up late." He rubs his eyes. "I volunteer at a soup kitchen on Sunday nights."

A soup kitchen – Rachel will love this. Her Mr. Perfect has a social conscience too.

"There was a fight between two of the regulars and I had to break it up. The cops came and I gave a statement at the station. Police type very slowly."

"So much for doing good."

"It's not usually like that." He scratches the stubble on his chin. "Mostly it's fun. It's a side of life I'd never normally experience and it's a good balance to this place."

"How long have you been doing it?"

"Three years, on and off." He rubs his hands together. "Now, I'm sure you're interested in my volunteering, but you're not going to avoid talking about why they booked you for an emergency session on your first day back."

Am I that transparent?

He waits for me to speak. The hum of his computer fills the room. I fiddle with my peace ring. "So," I clear my throat, "do you know about the Merapi Incident?"

From the way his eyes crinkle he could be holding in a smile. He shakes his head, so I tell him.

"Quite a story. Usually students sneak out to clubs, not volcanoes." He cups his chin and adopts his Dr. Freud pose. "What did you learn about yourself from the experience?"

Stokes wants me to have an epiphany. I look at my feet but my ugly school shoes are giving me nothing.

"Um, I'm a sucker for adventure."

Stokes nods.

"Sometimes I want to break the rules."

"Why?"

"Well, if I hadn't, I would've missed one of the best experiences of my life." I fold my arms. Surely that's enough self-reflection for one session.

"So you'll break the rules if you think it's worth it?"

"I guess." I gulp down some water and wipe my mouth.

"What else?"

"That Libby Hartnett is a certified bitch and has gone to war against me." I tell him about the Hash run and he grimaces when I show him the fading scabs from the insect bites on my arm.

"That was extreme provocation, but you held it together. That's great progress. How did you manage it?" He clasps his hands between his knees.

"Progress? Everyone talks like I'm crazy. I do have some self-control."

He holds up a hand. "Bad choice of words. I'm not everyone, Mel. I'm saying that would take a lot of self-control for anyone. There's strength in that. How did you do it?"

Faced with Stokes' patience, my spiky irritation fades. "I kept thinking about three strikes. I counted to ten a lot, though I usually only made it to five. And Rache was amazing. Sometimes she got angry for me, so I didn't have to."

"And the diary?"

"What?" I shift back in my seat and my heart thuds.

"Did you keep one?"

I blink at him, my cheeks burning.

"Thought you might have changed your mind, but I'm guessing my suggestion went nowhere?" he says.

"Suggestion?"

"To keep a diary."

"Oh no, diaries aren't my thing." I can breathe again but my heart is still pounding.

"So how do you feel about Libby now?"

"Can't stand her. That she had a go at Rachel too . . ." Stokes gives me a small nod. "I said nothing when I caught her smoking but she snitched on me to the teachers first chance she got. Everything I do I get caught, but she's so fucking evil and she gets away with everything." I cover my mouth with my hand – I've dropped the F bomb. "Sorry, Mr. Stokes."

He waves away my apology. "When I feel like that, I trust karma to take care of it. Sometimes it helps."

"In this case karma's on holidays," I say.

"But you don't know. That's the trick, to trust it even though you don't see it working. You don't know what else Libby might be going through."

The words of the wise man in Birkenstocks hang in the air. I think about Libby, triumphant at the end of the Hash, then miserable when she thought no one was watching. Libby saying goodbye to her aunt at the airport with real sadness in her eyes, and no parents there to farewell her.

"What is it, Mel?"

"I don't get it. Why's she so nasty? So angry?" I drag my fingers through my hair. "I don't want to understand her. It hurts my brain."

"You can never know what someone's demons are. God knows I've got mine, and I'm sure you've got yours."

I squirm. Maybe Stokes has Xray vision and can see my birthmark. He might know more about Libby than he's let on. He might have counseled her.

"What happened to Libby's mum?"

Knowledge ripples across his face, before he hides it. "You know that's confidential." His jaw is set.

I think of Libby's dad and how dominant he was at the circle meeting.

"What are you thinking?"

"Maybe she's human, at least a bit. Maybe she struggles with stuff and her dad and that's why she's so mean and tries to control everything. She's still a total bitch from hell though."

Stokes shifts forward and smiles. "This is a real breakthrough. You've found compassion for her in very challenging circumstances. I've counseled many people – adults included – who never manage that. It shows a lot of maturity on your part."

I look away.

"I mean it. It's too easy to think of people as good or bad. It's very powerful to walk in someone else's shoes."

I remember the fermented banana chunks in my sneakers and screw up my face.

We grow quiet but it's not awkward. Stokes has this way of paying attention without making you feel like he's dissecting you. But I know the drill. It's up to me to "direct the conversation" and there's no way I can beat the Zen master in a silence contest.

"Mum went ballistic about Merapi."

"Did she?"

"Yeah. I'm grounded until exams are over."

Stokes' pocket buzzes and he grabs at his phone. "Sorry about this, I have to take it," he says to me. "Hello?" He stands to take the call and motions for me to stay put before he slips out into the corridor and closes the door behind him.

I stare at the filing cabinet and run a finger under my collar. Stokes came too close before and this might be my only chance – I have to return the file. Possibility burns as I unzip my backpack and search inside it. My fingertips touch the metal edges of the file and the cool leather of the diary. I grab the file, crouch in front of the filing cabinet and pull on the drawer, but it sticks. Another tug, but it doesn't budge. The key isn't in the cabinet. My pulse throbs in my neck and I yank open his desk drawer. It's full of paper clips, staples, pens, protein bars, and pins that jab my fingers when I feel my way into the dark corners. I run my hand under the desk but there are no secret hiding places.

Stokes' voice reaches me through the closed door and I flinch. Where would he keep the key? I scan the desk again, shuffle through his in-tray, and flip his keyboard. Nothing. There's an antique breath mints tin tucked behind his monitor and it rattles when I grab it. The lid is stuck, but after a few attempts I twist it open and find two small keys inside. The first key doesn't fit the lock, but the second slides in and I yank the filing cabinet drawer open with my shaking hands. I heave the files toward me until I've created a gap at the back. I slide the file into place, but then I remember Oma's photo in the diary and snatch it out. When I return the keys to the tin the lid is too stiff. I clamp the tin and the lid together but they won't budge. After one last go

I shove the tin behind the monitor with the lid perched on top.

Please don't notice.

The doorknob turns and I bolt for my backpack, snatching it from where I've left it on the floor. When I turn around Stokes is in the room, his phone in his hand, his eyes fixed on me.

TWENTY-FIVE

My heart drums and my hands shake as I clutch my backpack. I keep my eyes on Stokes the whole time and pray he doesn't notice the breath mints tin.

"I can see you've guessed . . ." Stokes gestures to my backpack.

What the hell is he talking about?

"I'm sorry, Mel, but this will take longer than I thought. It's the police about last night. See you in a week, OK?" He runs a hand through his crumpled hair.

I straighten up and sling my backpack over my shoulder. My cheeks redden. "No worries. Catch you then."

I scoot out the door, up the hallway and all the way to the yard. I round a corner and collapse against a wall. The red bricks warm my back. I pant and wait until my heart stops going crazy.

That was way too close.

At recess Rachel and I hang out on the balcony above the library, which gives us both shade and sunshine. For some reason we're the only ones who use the balcony, apart from a sneaky teacher or two judging from the cigarette stubs in the corner. I stretch out my legs. My fawn standard-issue socks have dribbled down to my ankles.

"Guess what?" Rachel props herself up on one elbow.

"What? And why are we whispering?"

"It's more fun that way," Rachel whispers back. "I've got myself a date with Angus. You know, the cute one." Her eyes sparkle.

"That's cool!"

It was lust at first sight when Rache spotted Angus at a dance party in January but she hasn't mentioned him recently. She must have been plotting in secret.

"I got sick of waiting and asked him out."

The warning bell interrupts and we gather our books and descend the stairs. "You should come with us, do a double date with volcano guy."

"I'm grounded, remember?" I pout but I'm kind of glad. I don't need that pressure.

"Have you talked to him?"

"Not yet."

"Don't scare him off." She bounds down the last step and waits for me.

"He's just a friend."

Rachel grins at me. Sometimes she makes me feel like a freak because I don't have crushes on boys all the time. Well, ever really. I don't know if it's a girls' school thing, but Rache is always after someone. Last year it was my brother's mate Finn, and she wouldn't listen when I warned her he was a sleaze. It was the worst when I had to tell her he was cheating on her.

"You know this date with Angus means you're cheating on Stokes?"

She smirks. "How's it going with Couch Man anyway?"

"He thinks I've made progress." I laugh. "So you still haven't found a reason to go to him?"

"Nuh, would you believe it? For all my ingenuity I can't find an excuse that sounds believable. I can't do self-harm – I'm too squeamish – and no one would believe I've got an eating disorder."

"Maybe you want to admire him from afar," I say.

"Nope," she grins. "I want to be right up close."

We turn the corner and squint into the full glare of the sun. Some Year Nines walk by and check us out, then look away, but one girl flicks her dark ponytail and meets our eyes. She mutters something to the girl next to her who looks up at us and laughs before they barge through the library doors.

"Every year's got one." Rachel stares after the girl.

"Speaking of ours, what do you know about Libby's parents?"

"Why?"

"Just wondered."

"They split a couple of years ago. Her mum moved to the States." Rachel frowns for a moment. "Don't tell me you're feeling sorry for her?"

"I guess I can kind of understand why she might be angry."

"Oh, come on. I mean, I'm on my second stepdad, if you don't count the boyfriends Mum didn't marry, and I barely see Dad. And when I do he's like a zombie because of the baby, but do I go around acting like Libby?"

I think of Michael's mother – her death hadn't turned him into a psycho either.

"Shit happens, but it doesn't give you a licence to be a bitch," she says, her curls shaking.

The second bell rings.

"Yeah, I guess." I step back. "Better get to art."

"See you." Rachel strides toward the media studio, then spins around. "You know what she is?"

"What?"

"A poor little rich bitch, that's what." She disappears around the corner.

I grin. Maybe Rachel has just saved me from becoming a total sucker.

For a moment I feel ultra mature in the café with all the Fitzroy hipsters, but then a woman at the next table with a Cleopatra hairstyle and a dragonfly tattoo on her shoulder gives me a withering look, like I'm not cool enough to be there. I focus on the coffee dregs in my cup.

Michael breezes in. His hair's sticking out and he's messed up the buttons on his woven blue shirt so that one side hangs lower than the other. When he spots me he flashes me a huge grin.

"Hey!" I jump up to hug him, then second-guess myself and stumble over my chair. But he wraps his arms around me, setting something free in my chest. My ear is squashed against his collarbone and his heart beats strong and fast.

"I'm usually more graceful," I say over his shoulder.

"Yeah, I've seen you in action."

We pull apart.

"*Apa kabar*?" His eyes are shining, despite arriving at five this morning, two days later than planned.

I nod and sit down, battling the electric tension in my body. Too much coffee.

He struggles to fold his legs under the low table. A waiter appears and takes his order.

"So, how's it feel to be under house arrest again? You're like a political prisoner or something." He flicks a paper tube of sugar against the table.

"It sucks. But Mum's out until seven so it was ideal sneaky time." I grin.

He yawns and tries to hide it behind his hand. "Sorry. Still stuffed." He takes his Americano from the waiter and dumps two sugars into it.

"Hey, look what I found the other night." I pass my phone to him.

He opens the blog post and his eyes widen. "What? I don't believe it."

In a moment of excruciating boredom, while I was trying to read about conscription for Australian history and tangling myself up about Devi, I stumbled across this random profile on Lina, the singer in Yandra's band.

Michael's eyes light up. "Imagine if we could see her play here."

"It'd be epic. That was so much fun."

"Yeah. We had a lot of fun over there."

Our smiles hold for a long moment.

"Hey, let's celebrate your jailbreak. Cake?" he says.

A glass treasure trove of cakes is in my line of vision and there's a glossy lemon tart with my name on it.

"Mmm, lemon tart. But I've only got two dollars left . . ."

"We could split it?"

"Done. I'll order it on the way back from the restroom." I slip through the tight squeeze of tables, find the bathroom and freeze when I see my reflection in the mirror. I'm wearing a latte mo that spans the full width of my top lip. I groan – that's why Cleopatra gave me that look. I bend over the sink and rub it off.

I slink back to our table, minus the mo but with a slice of lemon tart. Within minutes we've reduced it to a faint smudge of yellow against the plate.

"This Devi thing has been driving me crazy. I've made zero progress. Zero. And I've heard nothing from Yuliana. It's the worst." I pull my hair back off my face and sigh.

"That sucks. What are we going to do? I think about her all the time."

"I know, but I've been working on it." I show him a photo of the clues on my wall from Devi's diary.

"Aren't we meant to be leaving it to Yuliana?" He looks up from my phone.

"Yeah. But I can't stand doing nothing . . ."

"Same. And we might find something that helps her," he says.

"Exactly. We'll be careful."

Michael studies the list and rubs his forehead. "Just like Jogja, hey?"

"Except this time I'm stuck."

"We'll crack it." He reaches under the table and pulls out a camera from his courier bag. "Hey, want to hunt down some graffiti with me?"

"What? Why?"

"Art project for school. If you don't want to, that's cool, it's not due til next term."

"Not those horrible tags." I screw up my face and dig at a dent in the wood grain on the edge of the table.

"Nah, hate that stuff, but I love stencils. And we're in the right neighborhood. Come on." He grabs my hand over the table.

We wander down Rose Street and into a laneway. It's a gritty tunnel of color with giant graffiti murals on both sides. Michael snaps away, propping himself up on the grotty cobblestones to achieve the right angle. Stencils are pasted over the top of some of the aerosol pieces. The trail continues down the lane and there are a few tags close to the ground. My pulse speeds up when I spot the distinctive curves and the slashing sweep of Siren's tag in angry red. I crouch down and study it.

Michael comes to a stop beside me.

"It's an old friend's," I say. Sarina's. There are splashes of mud on the wall, making it hard to tell if the tag is new or one from Year Nine.

Michael nods and we continue down the lane. "Hey, show me that list of clues again," he says.

I hand him my phone and he taps at it.

"What are you doing?" I try to peer over his shoulder.

"You forgot one." He flips the phone around so I can read the screen.

STOKES.

"Of course," I say.

"Does Devi mention Stokes at all? I only translated the bits you asked me to, not the whole thing."

I shake my head. We both sigh. My eyes drift back to my phone, to my list of clues and to Stokes. The letters seem to pulse against the blue screen. There's something edging around the corners of my mind, teasing me.

"I've got it."

"What?" He turns to face me.

"It's Stokes – we've got to follow him."

TWENTY-SIX

Stokes seemed pretty cool, but after following him for the last three nights I have my doubts. His life is so boring: work, supermarket, TV. Repeat. Yawn. Except last night he got wasted at the pub. But that's about it. He's living the life of a single guy and we haven't seen his wife at all – I can't help wondering about the woman in the photo on his desk.

"We're wasting our time, aren't we?" Michael's voice is flat. He pushes his sunglasses back on his nose.

"Don't worry. Something will happen." I put my heels on the seat and hug my knees.

"It's already been three nights and we're not getting anywhere. We should give up."

"We've got to keep trying. If nothing happens tonight we've still got tomorrow." I sneak a glance at the clock on the dashboard.

We're camped out in the back lane behind the teachers' car park. By day I'm sitting exams, by night I'm cramming and stalking Stokes. Mum's been cruisy since I hit the books and she has a stack of late-night bookings. Dad's in the Solomon Islands. So no one's checking on me.

Michael's taking the biggest risk. He learned to drive years ago but he's too young for a full driver's licence. If a cop pulls us over he'll be dead. Michael thinks that won't happen because it's an "old man's car." His brother, Jack, bought it from their grandpa.

My foot slides on the junk food wrappers on the floor. Subway, KFC, and Ali Baba. I pull the kebab wrapper off the underside of my shoe. It smells rank. We ate kebabs the first night we followed Stokes.

"Man, we're gross." Michael shakes his head.

"What are we going to eat tonight? McDonald's for a change?"

"You're thinking about food already?"

"Course." I flash a cheesy smile.

"Thai? I know a good place." His phone beeps with a message. "Shit. Jack's coming back tomorrow morning."

"But I thought—"

"Yeah, I know." He ruffles his hair. "Crap."

Jack's been in Tasmania on a field trip and Michael's been borrowing his car on the sly. With no car we'll be out of options.

"We'll get lucky tonight, I know it." I force a smile,

but it's all crowding in on me. Every day that we don't find Devi gnaws at my conscience. It's been too long since we found out her secret. How much longer can she survive? And still nothing from Yuliana. I chew on a nail. My Indonesian exam is tomorrow and I could do with another night of cramming. Every minute I spend chasing Stokes puts me at risk at school.

A flash of navy blue. Stokes' Subaru wagon turns out of the car park. I pull down my baseball cap and slide lower. Michael starts the Magna and we follow Stokes for a few minutes until he pulls up outside a stretch of patchy lawn in front of the pale towers of the Carlton Housing Estate. Stokes steps out of his car, flings his bag over his shoulder and walks down a path. Three small kids in school uniforms yell out to him. He turns around and waits for them to catch up. They walk down the path together, one girl skipping, all heads tilted up to meet Stokes' eyes, like he's a rock star. The group passes through a gate with a sign on it and enters one of the towers.

"Can you read that?" I say.

Michael squints and shakes his head. We jump out of the car and examine the hand-written sign: *Homework club, room 411.*

"Must be volunteering," Michael says.

I rub my neck and whimper. "I'm a shit person. When I

think of all the nasty things I was thinking about him . . ."

"You could still be right."

I point to the gate and shake my head. "No, I mean he volunteers at a soup kitchen too. He's seriously Citizen of the Year or something."

Michael shrugs and my conscience uses me as a punching bag.

The sky is ochre when Stokes emerges over an hour later, taking bites from the huge wrap in his hand. We follow him again and after ten minutes he turns into a YMCA car park, takes a bag and a squash raquet from his car and enters the gym.

"Subject exhibits signs of remorse after night on the piss," Michael says.

I snort. "Hey, you know what this means?"

"What?"

"Dinner." I grin at him.

It's dark when we return to the YMCA from the takeaway. We shovel noodles in fast and I'm nearing the bottom of my vegetarian pad thai when Stokes emerges, looking virtuous and flushed, and heads to his car. We follow him through narrow backstreets until he pulls up outside a house on the corner of a laneway. We watch him in the rearview mirror. He gets out of his car and looks around, like he's checking if anyone is watching. I hold my breath but he doesn't spot us on the other side of the street. He strides down a narrow laneway and disappears into the gloom.

We inch the car forward until we're level with the laneway and take the closest parking space. The lane's dark and it's impossible to see Stokes' destination from the car.

"I'll check it out." Michael's hand is on the car door.

"We'll check it out." I'm not going to be a passenger.

We enter the laneway and the night grows a few shades darker. Our footsteps on the greasy, uneven cobblestones make the lane sound hollow and abandoned. None of the houses front the lane. There are fences, the backs of sheds, and the sides of two-storey terraces. The lane's too narrow for cars.

Where did Stokes go?

A few yards ahead of us the lane makes a sharp bend. I point at the street sign – Bleak House Lane. There's nowhere else to go. On the corner there's a red brick double-storey terrace house covered with ivy. My pulse races and I grab Michael's arm. A burst of wind stings us and sways the tall ghost gum in the yard.

"That's the silver tree! Devi's in there—"

"This is it," he talks over me.

We turn the corner and hanging above a doorway there's a neon blue sign for *Little Heaven* with the illuminated outline of a reclining woman.

"Don't look, camera above the door," Michael says through tight lips. "Keep walking."

There's another camera in a black plastic dome further along the veranda and a security light snaps on as we pass. Blood pounds in my ears but we force ourselves to stroll down the street.

We walk to the end of the lane, turn left, and loop back to the street where we're parked. We stop and stare at each other.

"She's in there. As soon as we drove here I felt it." My breath rises in vapor clouds past his ears.

We climb into the car and the stale fish and soy sauce smells from our abandoned takeaway boxes hit me.

"It's definitely the place, it matches her descriptions. But how do we know she's in there?" Michael asks.

"What do you mean?"

"From what I've read they often move them around. From brothel to brothel."

I gulp. "So they could have moved her already?"

He shrugs.

The windshield is starting to fog up. I pull at my peace ring. "What if I go in there and say I'm . . ." My throat dries out. "Looking for work?"

"Are you insane? You want to pretend to be a hooker?" His eyebrows almost reach his hairline. "What if they ask you to audition?"

My face burns. "OK. Maybe that won't work." I check the time on the dashboard: 6.52. "But have you got a better idea? We're so close but we're running out of time. Mum'll be home at eleven."

And Jack will be home tomorrow.

The silence prickles between us. I rub the windshield until it squeaks and I've made a big hole in the condensation.

"I can't believe he went in there. It makes me sick." I pull a face.

"Does he seem sleazy? Creepy?"

"I always thought he was kind of admirable, you know?" I say. "I might be able to understand if he was really ugly, but he's not. Half the school has a crush on him. It's not like he needs to pay for it."

"Maybe he's got some weird sex fetish?"

"Ugh."

For weeks I've been denying the obvious link between him and the diary: Stokes goes to brothels. He must be seeing Devi for sex. Why else would he have her diary?

"What if . . ." Michael presses his hands together. "I go

in there? And pretend to be a customer."

His words hit me hard. I hide behind my hair to absorb them. Michael in a brothel. I don't like it. He wouldn't actually do anything, would he?

"It might work." I cross my arms.

He stares at me. "You think?"

I nod.

"I was hoping you'd say *no way*." He pushes back against his seat and scrapes his hair from his forehead. "I'd be too chicken."

I swallow a laugh. He catches me glancing at the clock again.

"We need to know if she's still in there, like you said." I shiver. "It's creepy but it's the only way."

Michael sighs, then jumps out of the car. I scramble after him.

"I'm doing this," he says, and turns for the lane.

I move to join him but he takes a step back. "You should stay."

I screw up my face. "I was just going to walk you down . . ."

"If Stokes comes out he'll recognize you. You can keep watch from the car."

I don't like it, but I can't argue with it.

He squares his shoulders and avoids my eyes. "Have

you got any money? I've only got sixty on my card."

I take a step back and my shoe crunches into a pile of leaves. "You want money?"

"It's not like I'm going to do anything, but they probably won't let me in otherwise."

"Oh." I rummage in my pockets and find my debit card. "It's got forty on it. Is that enough?"

"Shit, I don't know." He takes the card from my frozen hand and zips his jacket up to his chin. "Wish me luck."

"Just find Devi."

He disappears down the lane.

TWENTY-SEVEN

Through the windshield I watch the silhouettes of a couple eating dinner upstairs in a terrace house like it's a normal night. I chew my last nail and watch for Michael's lanky gait, but the mouth of the lane is empty. His unfinished box of noodles sits behind the gear stick. I try to ignore it, I've already scraped the bottom of mine. The radio jars with harsh advertising or depressing news. Michael's noodles loom, the box grows larger and larger in my vision. I sigh and demolish them in minutes.

I switch stations until the words of a song pound me. "*Losing your way, with all your dumb decisions . . .*" It's all about me, all my screw-ups since Year Nine and never being able to find my way back again. I'm ready for that familiar wave of shame, but nothing happens. Must be out of practice.

A sleek black car pulls up beside me and I turn the music down. The driver bends over the steering wheel and studies his phone. He makes a call and the glow from his phone illuminates his profile. In detective mode, I sneak some shots of him on my phone while he's talking. He's kind of hot, but he could be a brothel customer.

What's taking Michael so long? Maybe he's found Devi. My back is clammy and I open the window a crack. Cold air rushes in but my shirt's sticking to me. The man in the black car is still on his phone.

My breath catches and my eyes well up. Why am I so worked up? I try to take a deep breath but my chest is wheezy. It's the neon sign, the bars on the window, Stokes disappearing down that laneway. I wheeze again. My drink bottle is between the seats, next to the empty noodle boxes, and I slug down some water. There's marker scrawled on the side of the boxes: "V" and "S."

V for vegetarian.

S for seafood.

Fuck.

I start to shake. My tongue's fat and I lean forward and pant, the way the doctor showed me, and scratch at the door for the handle. I pull at it but it sticks until I find the central locking and the door falls open. Cold night air rushes at me and for a moment I can breathe. I tumble out and stagger to the trunk.

The trunk yawns open and I claw at the contents – school blazers, a soccer ball, a leather jacket. I spot the brown and blue of my bag. I yank the zips and search for my EpiPen with only the dull trunk light to help me. My lips are swollen, my throat's closing. I find it in the inside compartment. My hands shake and I drop the EpiPen and it rolls into some leaves at the back of the car. I fall to my knees.

Where the hell is it?

EpiPen, EpiPen. I claw at the leaves until I feel the hard plastic and seize it. I rip off the safety release but I'm shaking so much I can't hold it steady.

There's a figure next to me. "Are you alright?" he says.

But I don't look at him.

Can't breathe.

The blurred man grabs it from me. "I know what to do, don't worry," he says. "My sister's allergic to peanuts." He stabs my thigh with it, the way you're meant to. My heart screams and I can breathe again. I shut my eyes.

Michael's in front of me, his eyes immense, fierce. He holds my arms and shouts at the guy: "What the hell are you doing?"

The world's all pixellated. In seconds my heart finds its rhythm and gravity fills my feet again. I suck in air.

"It's OK." I turn to the guy from the car, ready to thank him.

"Are you alright? Do you need an ambulance?" The guy has to stoop to speak to me.

It's the first time I've seen him front-on and I blink, my vision still blurry. I shake my head and grip the trunk for support. I must be delirious because I've seen his face before.

In the diary.

TWENTY-EIGHT

After my near-death by pad thai Michael rushed me to the emergency department to get checked out. While we were waiting for a doctor he suggested going to the police and telling them what we knew.

Good idea.

Now I'm sitting beside Michael in the tatty waiting room of the Brunswick Police Station and doubt is swirling. He wanted us to see the cops yesterday, but after my exam and my Close Encounter of the Kurt Kind I couldn't face it. But today, even though every one of my bones feels sore and I hate police stations, I couldn't say no any longer.

I wriggle on the moulded plastic seat and resist biting my fingernails. There's a "wanted" poster on the wall for an armed robbery suspect – mug shots of a shaved head, broad face, piggy nostrils, and deep-set eyes under chunky eyebrows. No one looks that criminal in real life.

Or do they? A flash of Kurt's face. I flick through the photos on my phone and compare them to the drawings in my copy of the diary. It's definitely Kurt.

"I can't believe it either." Michael scratches the back of his neck.

I shiver when I get a flash of Kurt's fingers around my EpiPen. Helping me. It's all too much.

"I got this the other night." Michael shows me a photo on his phone: PQQ 263. "It's Kurt's license plate."

"You took that while I was turning into a puffer fish?" My voice rises.

"Before I knew you were. I was walking back, saw you two at the back of the car and thought it looked dodgy, so I took it."

When I got home from the hospital I called Dad but I couldn't get through. I try now and a recorded message plays in a language I don't understand, then the call drops out.

"Who are you trying to call?" Michael asks when I hang up after a second attempt.

"Dad. But he's in Burundi, I think, and I can't get through."

"Wow, you'd tell your parents about this?" he says.

"Not Mum. No way. She'd be more worried about me getting expelled than helping Devi. But Dad might even have worked with trafficking victims."

I put my phone away.

Michael jiggles his leg. He's been doing it ever since the young cop at the counter told us to take a seat.

"Stop it." I grab his knee.

He tucks his feet under the chair. At the brothel after he had worked up the guts to press the buzzer they kept him waiting for ages. When they finally opened the door, the security guards laughed in his face when he couldn't produce ID. If he'd been a year older they would have let him in.

Ick. Ick. Ick.

A skinny woman in her twenties is at the counter. Her hair is scraped back into a tight ponytail. She wants to cancel the intervention order she took out against her ex-boyfriend because this morning they got back together. The constable has a wispy moustache which moves up and down as he explains that it's not that easy. I tune out.

"How are we going to do this? They're never going to believe us, are they?" I grip the edge of the seat. "Excuse me, officer, we want to report someone for sex trafficking and, uh, here's our proof – a teenage girl's diary. But you can't read it because it's in Indonesian. Oh, and by the way, I stole it from the school counselor."

"Have you got another idea? We can't do nothing. We know we've got the right place."

Silence burns between us. I know I'm being a shit.

An older cop joins the younger one. He talks in low tones to the scrawny woman. She nods and begins filling out a form. He pushes his glasses back on his nose and glances up at us. My neck prickles. In slow motion I watch as his hazel eyes zoom in on me.

The fluoro lights shine on his badge but I don't need to read it to remember.

Sergeant Anderson.

I fly out of there, through the sliding doors so fast I almost hit them before they open. I race down Sydney Road, lungs heaving, and pull up outside a supermarket.

I've ruined everything.

Michael jogs toward me. "What the hell's going on?"

TWENTY-NINE

We're across the road at the A1 Bakery at the most private table I could find. That's not saying much. People are crammed into the place, wolfing down Lebanese pizzas and coffee with Saturday lunchtime abandon. It's loud with kids, a grass-stained teen soccer team, and big families gathered around tables. Voices bounce and chairs scrape across the tiled floor. The noise gives me a sense of protection.

There's a plate of spinach and cheese pie between us. It's total deliciousness but I can't eat. The past is rising like food poisoning. Michael has no such problem. He needs to know or he'll think I'm a crazy person, but once I tell him I've got to trust that he won't run out on me.

I clear my throat. "In Year Nine I got into a bit of trouble."

Michael puts down the pie. "What did you do?"

"I'm not proud of it. With my best friend, Sarina, I was seriously into street art. We'd get wasted and sneak out at night, spend hours in laneways and abandoned warehouses."

His eyes flash. "Did you get caught?"

"We were chased a few times, but we got away with it, for most of Year Nine."

"What was your tag?"

"Teflon."

He sniggers.

"Yeah, I was cocky." My mouth feels like chalk and I drain my glass of water. "We nicked supplies from small stores with crap security. Did it once, got away with it. It was addictive. We did it again and again. But after a while none of it gave us the same rush."

I keep my eyes down. Under the table I find a nasty glob of gum someone has left behind and pick at it.

"Then we did something really stupid. We broke into a house. Afterwards I freaked out. It wasn't like doing stencils in an empty laneway, we were in someone's home. Sarina was too into it. We did a second one but I told her that was it." I give up on the gum and glance up at him.

Michael's eyes are glued to me, his mouth parted.

"We never did another burglary but we shoplifted at one of the big chains. They got us good, called the cops."

People chat, kids squeal, spoons bang against tea cups, and the coffee grinder vibrates, but all the noise can't break through the bubble we're in.

"Sarina fucked up, she was wearing a ring from our last burglary when they caught us. She went down for it. I lied through my teeth, made out it was my first time, and I was lucky. That cop at the station, Sergeant Anderson, didn't believe me but I got away with it. He looked at me like I was total trash."

I wait in my little prison of guilt for him to say something.

"What happened to her?"

"She went to juvie."

"That's harsh."

"Kind of." I suck in a breath. "The thing is, she had a record. And that last house we burgled, there was this old man living there. When he came home and saw we'd broken in, he collapsed. Heart attack." My voice cracks. "He was in intensive care for ages, but he died a month later. He might have been OK if we hadn't . . ." I look away. A memory pierces my chest – photos of his children and grandchildren in polished silver frames, lovingly arranged on the mantlepiece and every spare surface in his living room.

Michael is silent. It's almost as bad as the moment – nearly two years ago now – when Mum and Dad met me at the police station and I told them everything, whispering so the police wouldn't hear. That hard, stony knot in my chest when Mum told me how ashamed she was of me. How she hadn't brought me up to be so callous. Dad saying little, his face saying everything.

"God, that's so much to deal with." His blue eyes are darker than I've ever seen them. "No wonder you were so down on the cops. But do you really think he recognized you?"

"Definitely. You saw him."

"He looked up at us, but I don't think he—"

"No. He totally did. His eyes locked on me."

Michael rubs his hand over his mouth. "We can't go back there?"

"You don't understand. When that old man died what we did was all over the news. They gave me a formal caution. It's on my file. Not likely to believe me, are they?" I pick up a napkin and start to shred it. "Do you think I'm a bad person?"

"I mean, it's not good, but I've done some dumb things."

"As dumb as that?"

"Different dumb."

He moves to take my hand then stops and rubs his palm against the table. "When I was fourteen sometimes I used to drive Dad's car. My life was hell when he caught me, but I'd probably have kept doing it otherwise. What if I'd crashed? What if I'd killed someone?"

"Me and Sarina did." I try to swallow but I can't.

"You don't know that. You messed up but I can tell you've beaten yourself up about it. I haven't known you long but I reckon *I know you.* You've worked so hard for Devi and that's not something a bad person does."

I want to wrap myself in his words and erase the past, but I can't.

"Now that Kurt guy," he continues, "that's real badness."

But Kurt helped me. I can't make sense of anything anymore. Maybe the world is one crazy mess. Michael's staring at me and I bite the inside of my cheek. Despite his words, is he judging me? Will everything be different between us now?

"Um, Mel," he says.

I brace for his words.

"You going to eat that?" He points to my neglected spinach pie.

"All yours."

He wolfs it down.

Michael steps through the automatic doors into the police station. They close with a quiet whoosh behind him. We picked the station closest to his house because I've never been to it. I perch on a concrete planter box opposite the door, on the edge of the car park.

The male cop behind the counter is barely older than Michael. From outside I watch him stamping something for a guy with bed hair and a black moon boot. There's a row of chairs to one side of the counter and a couple are sitting there, along with an old lady and two men.

I will the cop to stamp faster.

Moon boot hobbles out of the station. The couple jump up and talk to the cop for a while, then sit back down.

Michael pulls his copy of the diary out of his backpack and it feels weird that I'm not beside him – but I can't risk it. He talks, his hands waving. The cop studies the diary and frowns. Michael points at the diary and the cop examines the page closely. The cop's lips move, then he rubs his hand over his mouth as he listens to Michael. He says something and ducks out through a back door.

A car speeds into the car park and five guys in their late teens spill out. Their basketball tops are torn and they've got cuts and marks on their faces. They burst through the doors to the station and swarm the counter. One of them bangs the bell with his palm. Everyone in the waiting area stares at them.

The cop reappears and the basketballers press up against the counter. He holds his hands out to them. *Calm down*? The cop passes Michael some paper and a pen. Michael edges down the counter and starts to write.

The old lady and one of the men are now at the counter, trying to get the cop's attention. One of the basketballers kicks his foot up in the air and points. He's in socks. Three of them don't have shoes on. His mates crowd up behind him, nudging Michael further down the counter. The cop drags his fingers through his hair, looking overwhelmed.

Michael is slumped next to me on the planter box.

"We could come back when it's quiet?" I say.

"He thought I was full of shit." His mouth is all pinched.

"But he got you to fill in a report. That's –"

He shakes his head. "It sounded so stupid when I told him. Even I didn't believe it."

I pull at my lip. "They might still ring you. When they read your report, when it's less busy."

"They think I'm delusional." Michael checks his phone, his face tense. "Look, I've got to babysit Dan. Catch you later?"

He slings his backpack over his shoulder and walks away, his head hanging. He doesn't look back. I watch him until he turns the corner. I've never seen Michael so down. I've got no clue what to do next and my past has ruined everything.

Dead leaves crumple under my feet on my walk to the tram stop. I kick up their remains. I'm glad I told Michael the truth, but did he just run away from me? Maybe I'm being paranoid but when he was still with me it was easier to believe that nothing had changed between us.

THIRTY

The clock on the wall ticks, the minute hand pushes toward three. We grip our pens and race to fill the pages with last-minute insights about *Lolita*. Ms. Moss walks between the rows of desks and glances at the clock.

"Time, girls. Pens down." She clasps her hands together and scans the room.

All around me pens clatter on desks and chairs scrape the vinyl floor. I lace my fingers together, stretch my palms toward the ceiling, and share a smile with Rachel. My exams and my house arrest are over. We line up at Moss' desk to hand in our papers and file past her.

Outside, the cool air carries me to freedom. Rachel stands against the red brick wall, looking spaced-out. Her face lights up when I approach.

"How'd you go?" I yawn so hard I sway backward.

"Alright. You look stuffed."

"I'm beyond tired, but my house arrest is finished. Done." I let out a whoop.

She beams back at me. "Finally."

Rachel links her arm in mine and we stroll toward the locker room.

"Hey, how was your last date with Angus? You never told me."

"It was fun, another nice date . . ." She twists a button on her blazer.

"But?"

She scans the area outside the locker room and steps closer to me. "He didn't make a move. It's driving me crazy. He's so cute."

"What's stopping you?"

"I'm trying to go slow for once." She grins and pushes the locker room door, holding it open for me. "Hey, let's celebrate. Want to go to Gelo Bar? We could make ourselves sick."

"I've got to see Stokes." I rub the back of my neck.

"Lucky you. What about later?"

"Sorry, promised I'd meet Michael."

She enters the security code for her locker. "OK then."

"I'll message you later."

She mumbles something with her head hidden behind her locker door.

There are hidden depths in the marmalade-colored carpet, details I've never noticed before. I track every twist and turn in the pile and drag my feet, but I still reach Stokes' door too fast. I've got no idea how to handle this. Will I be able to look him in the eye? I pause at his door. Should I come clean? Ask him outright why he has the diary? Yeah, right. But the instinct to tell him is strong, I'm so used to doing it.

I knock on the door. Silence. I knock again and wait, then ease the door open. His office is empty but his desk chair is twisted at an angle, like he's left in a hurry. The retro clock above his desk tells me I'm eight minutes early.

The photo of his wife has disappeared. My chest feels tight. Stokes is married. Stokes has sex with a trafficked girl. Who is the man I've been talking to all these weeks? I sink into his chair. There has to be an explanation, one that fits the man I know. We saw Stokes enter the laneway but not the brothel. He might have gone somewhere else. I spin clockwise in his chair. But there was nowhere else to go. It was all sheds, fences, and dead ends. Little Heaven was the only option. I spin the other way and crash against a stack of correspondence in his in-tray.

"Crap!" I catch the papers and straighten them in my lap. There's a letter on the top from St Michael's College.

It's a few weeks old and acknowledges "his recent job application." What, is he leaving Chis? I peek at the letter underneath but it's from the Australasian Guidance and Counseling Association thanking Mr. Ryan Gerald Stokes for agreeing to speak at their next conference.

Gerald – how embarrassing. It's nearly two, so I flick through the pile at speed, but find nothing more from St Michael's. I read the first and second letters again. Bile rises in my throat. I launch from the chair and run out of the room. At the end of the corridor Stokes appears.

"Hi Mel." He's puffing. "Unavoidably delayed. Let's start now." He gestures for me to follow him to his office.

I put a hand over my mouth. "I don't feel well. I'm going to see the nurse."

I can sense his eyes watching me as I rush down the hallway. Out of the building, I run straight past the nurse's office. The schoolyard is deserted. When I reach the locker room I grab my backpack and lock myself into the disabled bathroom. My hands tremble when I find the final entry and reread the clue that I overlooked a week ago.

When Mariska said Mr. Gerald was a good man, I dared to hope, but hope is poison. Mr. Gerald hasn't returned.

THIRTY-ONE

The cat is headbutting my thigh. I groan and force my eyelids open. The day is still dark, with only the first gentle light in my room. But I'm fully awake now. Mission accomplished, Hedy turns to the spare mattress on the floor and stalks Rachel's sleeping form. She nuzzles against Rachel's side and Rache wriggles in her sleep.

When I rub my eyes, last night's party smudges on my fingertips. With Devi on my mind I wasn't sure I'd have any fun, but it was one of the best parties I've ever been to, if not *the* best. Michael's dad threw this horror-themed thing and because he's a museum curator he had all these wild props. Like an ancient Egyptian mummy. Crazy.

Rachel mutters in her sleep. She likes Michael, even if she has the wrong idea about us. Though when a waitress flirted with Michael it felt weird, and not in a good way. So maybe Rachel does have the right idea. I push the thought aside.

Light builds behind the curtains. I grab my phone and scroll through my emails but there's nothing from Yuliana. I don't get it, I emailed her after we found the brothel but she hasn't responded. I send another message and my heart trips when a minute later my phone pings with a new email.

From Yuliana.

I'm out of the office at a conference. I'll respond to your message when I return.

Damn, damn, damn. I was so sure she was going to help us.

"Has someone died or proposed?" Rache says, sitting up.

I jump. "Huh?"

"Your face, you should see it. What the hell happened?" Rache crawls toward my bed.

"Nothing." I shove my phone into my sheets. "What a great night, hey?"

"That Jack, phew." She climbs on to my bed and fans herself.

Rachel was drooling over Michael's older brother all night. It was almost embarrassing, but I didn't say anything – that's just Rache. It gave me a chance to get Michael alone, tell him about Mr. Ryan Gerald Stokes and brainstorm our next move.

But we're stuck.

"Think you could line up a double date with him?" she asks.

"But Jack's seeing someone."

"Yeah, but Michael said he could be single any second." She tries to tame her bed hair with her fingers.

"God, Rache. What about Angus? Weren't you in love with him two seconds ago?"

"In lust. And I don't want to miss my chance with Jack."

I roll my eyes.

"Jeez. You're acting like Mum's uptight mates." She turns up her nose at me. "So what's up? Are you in trouble?" She edges closer and her eyes fall to my stomach. "You're not?"

"You're so off the mark."

"What's going on then?"

Shit. Since we returned to Melbourne I've barely seen her. My house arrest, exams, and following Stokes have consumed all my spare time. Apart from having lunch together I've been avoiding her, although I didn't realize it until this second. Rachel is too perceptive, she knows something went down in Indonesia but she hasn't bugged me about it. But now her big browns are trained on me, waiting. I let out a big sigh and the whole story about Devi tumbles out.

"We found the brothel. Look at this." I show her the photos of Kurt on my phone and Devi's sketch of him from the diary.

Rachel stares at the drawing. "Jesus Christ! And why the hell did Stokes have the diary?" Rachel grips my phone. "Makes no sense. It's not like she was a student?"

Her face is too close to mine.

"I don't know." I shrug and tug at the corner of my pillow.

"You're a crap liar."

"You're not going to like this . . ." I grip my peace ring like it has some magical power to defuse the situation. "I think she gave the diary to him, hoping he'd help her."

"But why? How do they even know each other?"

I suck in a big breath. "Stokes is . . . her customer."

Rachel flinches. She shakes her head and curls fall into her eyes. She blows them away. "No. No, you're wrong. He wouldn't do that."

"I wish I was. But I don't think so."

Rachel struggles to her feet. "You always do this. You have to find something wrong with everyone I like. I'm so fucking sick of it."

I stare at her. "What are you talking about? You can't seriously think anything would happen with Stokes."

She hurls my phone and it hits my thigh. I wince and she runs from my room, slamming the door. A second later she reappears, storms over to the spare mattress, snatches her stuff and burns out of the room again.

All without looking at me.

THIRTY-TWO

Any ideas?

Michael's message shakes me out of my mood. I'm on the tram with the model of a genome sequence that I made for science balanced on my knees. We've been volleying messages back and forth, but we're struggling. Devi's still trapped, there's been no news from Yuliana, and my past isn't helping.

No. Nothing.

I've been trying to blank out my fight with Rache. But on the walk home from the tram stop I can't help it anymore. Our fight still hurts, and I don't know how to fix things with her. This must be about Finn, her boyfriend from last year. It sucked telling Rache he was cheating, but why get pissed at me for it? Maybe it's not just about me killing her crushes – Rache was already a bit pissed at me for not spending so much time with her lately. Thank God the school holidays are coming, otherwise I'd be eating lunch alone in the library for weeks, even though it's not my fault she crushed on a wife-cheating-brothel-creeper.

Ever since Rache stormed out I can't stop thinking about Stokes. Stuff the agreement, I'm never having another session with him. There's no way I can sit and listen to his goodie two-shoes act when I know he's a total creep. Then I remember the kids greeting him at the homework club and how he helped me. How can he do that and then exploit Devi?

A tight band presses around my forehead. Devi, Rache, Stokes. They're my axis of angst and I keep bouncing between them like a masochistic pinball.

When I reach our gate I spot Dad's mud-encrusted boots outside the front door. I'd forgotten he was due home today from wherever. I walk faster. Dad will know what to do.

In the kitchen there's a note for me on the counter: *Mel, curry in the fridge for dinner. At the refugee meeting in Sunshine. Home late. Love Dad.*

I call him anyway, but it goes straight to voicemail and I hang up. This isn't something I can explain in a message. I'm glad my parents aren't clingy, but right now they're treating this parenting business a bit casually. At the moment I wouldn't mind having a wise elder to talk to and I guess you could put them in that category.

Theoretically.

Still half-asleep, I wrap myself in my dressing gown and stagger downstairs. Mattresses and lumpy shapes cover the living-room floor. I rub my eyes. The rise and fall of sleeping bodies comes into focus. They look Sri Lankan or Indian. There are two young boys, a teenage girl, a man and a woman in their early twenties, and another couple in their thirties. A small baby wriggles on one of the mattresses between the younger couple. A couple of the men snore, droning like lawnmowers.

I close the door and shuffle into the kitchen. Dad's at the stove, looking certifiable with his hair sticking out at weird angles. He's beating eggs in a huge steel bowl.

"Dad."

He jumps and swings around to look at me. There are charcoal rings under his eyes.

"You look like shit," I say.

"Morning, Ms. Sweetness and Light."

"What the hell, Dad?" I press my hands against the counter. "Who are those people? I nearly fell over them. What if I'd come downstairs half-dressed? Or naked?"

"Calm down," he says, scratching at his morning

stubble. “I didn’t have a chance to tell you. They’re Sri Lankan refugees. They’re our guests.”

“For how long? And when did you turn our home into a refugee camp?” I scowl at him.

Dad drops the whisk and it clangs against the side of the bowl. “You’ve got so much. Can’t you share some of it? At least pretend to be gracious.” He pours the eggs into a frying pan.

My shoulders are in knots. It’s tough competing with refugees for his attention. Sometimes I just want him to be my dad, not the world’s savior. I want to storm out and slam the door, but I think of Devi and I know I can’t.

Dad’s rifling through the fridge. I hover behind him. “Dad, there’s something I need to ask you.”

“Can it wait? It was a late night and I’ve got seven mouths to feed out there.” His tone softens. “Give us a hand?”

My dressing-gown pocket vibrates with a message from Rachel. This is either going to be an olive branch or a hand grenade, there’s no in-between with her. *Sorry ☹ Still feel funny but let’s forget it, kay? Come round tomorrow?*

“Can you fix the toast, Mel?”

I start to reply to Rache.

“Or get some plates at least?” Dad adds.

“Huh?” I keep typing.

“Don’t put yourself out,” Dad says. He turns his back on me and moves to the toaster.

“What? What do you want me to do?”

The baby cries and a voice calls out from the living room. Dad steps toward them, his hand on the door, his arm full of plates. For a moment he hesitates, but then he’s gone.

THIRTY-THREE

"Dad could never live in a building that didn't have a history," Michael says.

Their huge apartment is in a former chocolate factory, but now the essential oils factory next door perfumes the building. The scent of orange oil wraps around us like a blanket.

We're sprawled on the astroturf lawn on the rooftop, eating Tim Tams and avoiding Jack and Dan's epic *Space Invaders* battle downstairs. Their dad brought home an old arcade game.

Despite the churning clouds overhead I can't stop smiling. The school holidays begin in days and I've dodged the madness at home this afternoon. When I think about my fight with Dad, I reach for another Tim Tam.

My phone vibrates with a new email and I jerk upright.

"What is it?" Michael frowns.

"Yuliana."

He swings himself up and reads over my shoulder.

Dear Melati

My deepest apologies for my delayed response. I kept hoping to have good news. It hasn't been easy.

The day you left I visited Devi's parents. At first they would not believe me, even when I showed them the copy of the diary. They thought it was a cruel prank. It was awful to watch them struggle with the truth, but in the end they couldn't deny it. In their hearts they knew something was wrong and that Devi would have contacted them by now.

We went to the police, who were deeply suspicious. They seemed to think Devi had run away with someone and was telling lies to cover her tracks. It has taken many visits to convince them that she is missing. With your news about the brothel they're finally taking us seriously. Yesterday they told us they've opened an investigation - which is good news - but they wouldn't give us any more details. At last we have progress, but we're trying not to hope too much.

I'm finding it hard to sleep for thinking about Devi. It is agony for her parents.

Please don't do anything more – you have taken too many risks. I pray for Devi and I pray for you and Michael. I'll be in touch as soon as I have news.

Sincerely, Yuliana

I stare at the screen. A pulse beats in my neck. Yuliana is trying to downplay it but things are happening. The news about the brothel gave the police something real to work with. Not just a diary and a missing girl, but a place.

"This is good. They're on to it now, they're helping—"

Michael runs a hand through his hair and frowns. "What if one of them's in on it?"

"The cops?"

He nods. "It would explain why they took so long. Would be hard to get away with it without involving the cops."

"They wouldn't . . ."

He shrugs. "Some of them are dodgy, there's a lot of corruption."

I feel hideously naïve. It didn't occur to me not to trust the cops. I thought all of our problems were solved.

Shit.

"If Devi's traffickers find out, they might go after Devi's family." I hug my legs.

"Or Devi," Michael says.

I shake my head.

"Hey, I might be wrong." Michael nudges me with his shoulder.

"Those cops never rang you?"

"No." He sighs.

"We've got to try another station." I take a deep breath. "We're doing it. Tomorrow."

Michael's hair falls over his brow. "Third time, hey?"

"Yeah, maybe Fitzroy." A smile tugs at the side of my mouth.

He peers at me. "You're smiling. Thank God, you looked so freaked out."

"I was. I am."

He smiles back at me and there's such a sweet expression in his eyes that I have to look away. His eyes follow me as I reach for my bag and find the micro-USB Samuel gave me two years ago. I slot it into my phone and the album appears.

"You wanted to see my etchings?" I wriggle closer to Michael. I need something to distract me from thinking about tomorrow.

His face brightens and he flicks through my work. They're all gone now, destroyed by the weather or covered by other people's pieces. When all the shit went down in Year Nine, Mum and Dad made me throw out all my equipment – cans, markers, knives, and adhesive sprays. I knew I had to give it up, I didn't want to be tempted again, but it hurt to lose everything. Weirdly, Samuel understood. While I was grounded he photographed my work before it disappeared. It's the nicest thing he's ever done for me.

My old pieces bloom on the screen. Was that really me? It was so much fun – that electric thrill of working against the clock to throw our work on the wall and get away in time. Why did we have to push it too far?

Michael holds up the screen. "I love this."

It's my favorite; two girls tumble in the shape of the Yin and Yang symbol. One girl swims down, the other rises to the surface. One has light hair, the other dark. I squint, and realize it's Sarina and me. How did I never see that before? Year Nine was such a mess, there wasn't much time for contemplation.

"You've got mad skills. You shouldn't have given up."

I try to hide my smile. "Thanks."

"Why don't you do it again?"

"Kind of . . . painted myself into a corner, I guess."

He groans and I giggle. Then he zooms in on a detail. "Teflon. Is that a pitchfork for the 'T'?" I nod and smirk at my private joke. Michael passes my phone back to me.

"Seen Strokes?"

"You mean Stokes." I grimace.

He grins. "Nope. Strokes suits him better."

"That's gross." I whack his arm.

We laugh, our faces close together, until we pull back and rearrange ourselves. There's this prickly static between us now. Once hanging out with Michael was cruisy, but now I'm always hyperaware of the perimeter of my body and his distance from me. Every movement is self-conscious and heightened. Something shifted when we stalked Stokes, but the chase consumed us. Now when I don't see him for a day I get this jittery feeling. And when I do see him everything is more vivid. I laugh easier, but nervous energy fizzes in my veins.

Michael stretches out on to his side and props himself up on his elbow. His shirt gapes open for a moment and I catch a glimpse of the muscles across his chest. When did he get those? Ever since Borobodur I've thought of him as lanky, skinny even. I sneak another look. His upper body is like a surfer's with that v-shape from his ribs to his shoulders.

Oh, crap.

I cross and uncross my legs and turn my peace ring round and round. He listened to my crazy story about a diary, didn't judge me for stealing it, and gave up his nights to help me and Devi. He knows the worst – all my secrets.

And he's still here.

Michael says something and I watch his mouth without taking in what he's saying. I scramble forward and kiss him. His lips don't move.

I sit back on my patch of astroturf and can't bear to look at him.

"Mel . . ."

From the corner of my eye I can see that he's sitting up, his back ramrod straight. I'm dying inside.

He edges closer, reaches for me and we kiss again. His hands hold my face and his mouth is wide and soft. I curl my hand around his neck and we press as tight as we can get. My face and the back of my head are tingling, and my fingers thread through his hair. The kiss stretches on and on and on.

THIRTY-FOUR

"Aw, gross! You two are disgusting!"

We wrench apart. Dan is at the top of the stairs, grimacing at us.

"What do you want?" Michael says.

"Jack's on the phone to some girl." He rolls his eyes. "Play *Space Invaders* with me?"

Michael glares at him.

He snickers. "She's only kissing you because she feels sorry for you. Because you're ugly." Dan bolts for the stairs.

"You little shit." Michael races after him. Feet pound the steel steps and there's a squeal. Someone yells and bodies bash into the stair rail. A door slams. Silence.

Michael reappears, his face shiny and flushed. It's hard to meet his eyes now Dan has mangled the moment.

"Sorry about that." He gives me a lopsided smile.

We kiss again, but something isn't working. Our teeth collide and our mouths are out of sync. We try to keep going but it's not working. We pull apart.

I stand there looking everywhere but at Michael. It's cold on the rooftop now and I run my hands up and down my arms. I've kissed guys before, but always when I was half-wasted. When it didn't really matter. But never like this, never with someone like Michael.

"Um, that was . . . yeah," Michael says.

I risk a glance at him. He meets my eyes and tries to smile but his mouth can't manage it.

"I better run." I scoop up my backpack and rush toward the stairs.

"Mel, you don't have to," he says.

"Bye. Um, thanks for the Tim Tams."

My shoes are deafening on the steel stairs as I run down them.

Thanks for the Tim Tams. Mel, you idiot.

THIRTY-FIVE

A gigantic banner for *A Day in Pompeii* stretches above the entrance to the Melbourne Museum. It's the last day of school before the break. I love the museum – its soaring steel roof and vast dimensions make me feel like a tiny figure in an architect's model. But even our excursion can't cheer me up today.

Downstairs in the vulcanology exhibit memories of Merapi and Michael rush back. I pull out my phone and shoot Michael a message before I can second-guess myself: *Hi. Sorry I left like that. Have I stuffed up everything? Miss you.*

I almost feel like talking to Rache about this. At least she's got experience, but she's on the Media Studies excursion with Shanti.

Stop obsessing, Mel.

Justine has her hands pressed against a glass display, staring at the contents. Chis girls are crowding around her and I can't see anything. I wander into the next room. A dense silence fills the space. The crowd has thinned out, there are a few Chis girls scattered around, and I sit in the shadowy circumference of the exhibit. Violet light shines on a circle of plaster casts on a platform. A dog strains against a chain. A tiny boy lies on his back, his arm raised to shield his face. Two dying girls cling to each other. The plaster images revolve in a macabre carousel. Shackled, trapped, no chance.

I've been wasting time brooding about Michael while Devi's still a prisoner. But what the hell am I supposed to do? It's not like I've got superpowers.

I bolt out of there and find the restrooms. I need to throw water on my face and lock myself in a stall. For a few hours. I shove the door open. There's a mirrored wall and I blink hard against the glare of a row of bright lights. Two Chis girls are huddled together in front of the sinks. My skin prickles hot-cold.

Marnie has her hand on Libby's shoulder.

"She's not c-coming, she . . ." Libby chokes, her head down.

"Aw, Libs."

"Fuck. Sorry, you don't need this." She sniffs.

Marnie hugs her.

I'm frozen. They haven't noticed me yet. Can I back

away without making a noise?

"It's her work, says she can't ... and ... wants to fly me over, but Dad won't let me." Her voice breaks. "They don't give a shit about me, it's all about them."

Big, ugly sobs overpower her. Marnie rubs her back. As I step backward Marnie spots me. Her eyes widen and she mouths *get out.*

I wobble out of the bathroom. Libby doesn't cry. Ever. She's invincible. I didn't think she could even produce tears.

After school Rache and I sit on her back deck, drinking cups of chai. Rastas, her dog, lies next to us in a lazy, shaggy heap. Rachel is moaning about her mum dragging her to yet another fundraiser for the women's shelter. "It's a performance of the *Vagina Monologues*, can you believe it?" Her face twists. "Can you think of anything more gross? All these women on stage talking about their pussies. The set is a giant pussy too."

I laugh. "Go be a feminist, Rache."

"Why don't you go with Mum then? I'll chill at your place. We can swap."

"You and the seven and a half refugees Dad's taken in."

Rachel slams her mug on the deck. "You're not serious?"

"Totally."

We avoid the topic of Stokes. I ask Rachel for the latest about Angus.

"Saw him two nights ago, the absolute worst night of my life."

The back door swings open and Mrs. OBB emerges with a teapot. She tips tea leaves into the compost and smiles at us. "Hi girls. Didn't know you were out here. What you up to?"

"I'm telling Mel about the other night. Who hooked up, that sort of thing."

"Lovely," Mrs. OBB says absently, and the screen door bangs shut behind her.

I sit up and twist my peace ring. Mrs. OBB would be the perfect person to confide in with all her experience working with abused women. But I can't chance it, Rachel has just started talking to me again.

"At the movie we were at the back of the cinema," Rachel goes on, sipping her chai. "He's looking totally hot. I'm dying for him to kiss me and finally, *finally* he makes a move." She twists her mouth to one side.

"And?" My eyes are wide.

She squeezes Rastas' face in her hand. "Your kisses are less slobbery than his."

"Oh no."

"Oh yes." Rachel sighs.

"Can you train him?" I rest my cheek on her shoulder.

"He's not a dog, he's beyond training."

"Don't you think kissing can get better?"

"Nuh-uh." She shakes her head. "It's there or it's not."

I don't know where it is with Michael. Yesterday one moment it was amazing and the next I was running out of his place. I'm too embarassed to talk about it, even though it would make Rache feel better. It's too private. Why couldn't it be like kissing in the movies, except without the pouring rain and cheesy dialogue?

"Look, this diary thing . . ." Rache fiddles with her mug. "You're wrong about Stokes, there's no way—"

"But we saw him—"

She raises her hand. "I know, I know. But I don't believe it, OK?"

"I don't want to either."

"Let's forget about it," she says.

I breathe out.

She stands up. "C'mon, enough deep conversation. I've got a bag of chips inside."

"Now you're talking."

In the living room we flop onto the worn violet couch and rip open the jumbo bag of chips. With Rachel's step-siblings out for once, her house is peaceful. Mrs. OBB talks on the phone and clatters around the kitchen. The hot sweet scent of baking fills the living room.

"Libby was there, you know. At the movies."

"She was crying at the Pompeii thing." I take a handful of chips.

"Really? What about?"

"Only heard a bit. Think it was her mum canceling on her." I crunch through my chips. "It was horrible. Almost made me forget how mean she can can be."

"She used to be nice . . ." Rachel licks the orange coating from her fingers. There's still a dusting of orange crumbs on her top lip.

"Yeah?"

"We were kind of friends once." She glances away from me.

"Are you messing with me? Why didn't you tell me this before?"

"Excuse me, you're having a go at me for not telling you things?" She gives me a death stare. "And I said kind of friends, not actual friends. But honestly she was different and back then we were all friends." She wipes the cheesy bits off her lip. "Until Year Nine when her mum ran off."

Mrs. OBB sweeps into the room with a tray of hot muffins in her oven-gloved hands. "Libby took it hard, poor kid." She sets the tray on the coffee table. "Hungry?"

We take a steaming muffin each and I bite straight into mine, discovering oozing white chocolate and raspberries.

"So good," I say.

"Don't get the wrong idea, she never does this," Rachel says. "It's just for show."

Mrs. OBB dusts crumbs off her oven gloves.

"You were good friends with Libby's mum then, weren't you, Mum?"

Mrs. OBB shakes her head, the henna streaks in her hair shimmering. "We'd say hello at school things, but that was it."

"But I saw her at the shelter once. You were hugging her."

"Don't think so." She checks her watch. "I've got to fetch the twins. Leave them some muffins, OK?" She pulls off her oven gloves and rushes out the front door.

"That's weird," Rache says when she's gone.

I grab another muffin and pull off a crusty bit.

"It was definitely Libby's mum." She chews.

"Maybe she was just visiting the shelter or something."

She stops chewing and that arrowhead frown appears. "Only clients and Mum's really good friends know where the shelter is. For security reasons."

"So?"

"I always assumed they were friends, but . . ."

"You mean . . ."

Rache nods. "She must have been a client."

Oh. My. God.

Mr. Hartnett is a wife beater? Wife beaters are hard men with tattoos, bad singlets, and mullets, not pompous judges in blazers.

"Do you think he hit Libby too?" I ask.

Rache shrugs. "He might not have hit them. Mum says some men aren't violent, they're really controlling instead."

During the circle meeting Libby's dad seemed like he cared about her. But he did most of the talking. Libby was like a different girl. Everything I thought I knew about her has been thrown up in the air. I've got a taste of what it must be like in Libby's world and I almost feel guilty for hating her.

THIRTY-SIX

By the end of the tram ride home I've psyched myself up to try the police again. Bugger the caution on my file, there has to be a way to persuade them. Michael and I will try another station.

But things are still awkward between us.

Damn.

Hours after I sent Michael my message he responded with: *All good. Catch you later.*

I messaged back: *Sounds good.*

He responded with a thumbs up. We've messaged since then, but we haven't seen each other.

There's definitely something wrong with me. I make up with Rache and then I run out on Michael. I'm like a human conflict zone.

Sigh. It's all too hard.

I march up our garden path. Dad made me promise to come straight home after Rache's. I don't know what's up, but maybe I can try him again. I'll have to act like the perfect daughter and wait until he has a beer in his hand, but it's worth a go. Maybe he can go to the cops with me.

I swing the front door open and stare at the transformation. Our guests have covered the dining table and lounge furniture with the beautiful fabrics Dad has collected on his travels. They're carrying dishes of curries, pickles, lentils, and spiced pastries from the kitchen. A young woman with perfect posture holds a huge bowl of golden rice on one hip and balances a baby on the other. I move to take the rice from her, but she gives a quick shake of her head and glides by.

Dad is in a corner of the lounge, his grin as wide as mine. A man in his thirties approaches us. He's tiny, but appears to be the elder of the group.

"To thank you for your kindness. Please." He pulls out our seats and gestures toward the feast with his elegant hands.

We sit down and they serve us, creating huge mountains of rice, lentils, and curry on our plates, topped off with chutneys and pickles. They don't want to sit with us, but Dad insists and we feast together. Apart from the man who spoke to us, the group doesn't know any English, but we smile a lot and pass food back and forth. The woman with the baby teaches me the names of each dish and my clumsy attempts at Tamil make them giggle. I keep it up, happy to play the idiot to make up for my crappy attitude.

My phone vibrates against my hip and Dad skewers me with a glance. I ignore the call. It's not until eleven when, loaded with curry, I climb the stairs and remember to check my phone.

One missed call. A number I don't recognize. I listen to my voicemail: "Hi Melati, it's Agent Rose Hanna from the Australian Federal Police. Please call me back as soon as possible. We're hoping you can assist us with an investigation we're conducting with the Indonesian police. Thank you."

THIRTY-SEVEN

Oh. My. God. A cop wants to talk to me? My heart misfires.

Maybe the federal police are nicer than the Victorian ones. My finger hovers over her phone number, but it's too late to call her now.

Isn't it?

Just do it. This is what you wanted. But then I get a flash of Sergeant Anderson, the way he looked at me. I square my shoulders and call Rose Hanna's number.

Straight to voicemail.

I'm pre-verbal when my phone rings.

"Melati Nelson?" says a clear, smooth voice. "I'm Agent Rose Hanna."

My eyes snap open.

"Can you talk?"

Barely. It's 7.30, the earliest I've ever been awake on the first day of the school holidays.

"Yeah, no problem." I sit up so fast I bash my head against the headboard. I rub the sore spot and blink at the morning.

"Did Yuliana fill you in?" she says.

My heart flutters in my chest. I ease myself out of bed. Think of Devi, think of Devi.

"Only that the Indonesian police started an investigation," I say.

"We're working together on this. Yuliana tells me you think you know where Devi is?"

I tell her about following Stokes and finding Kurt. She listens without interrupting, apart from the occasional *go on* and *let me get that down*. She's sussing me out, I guess. Cops must hear from plenty of delusional freaks. I'm glad she can't see my Simpsons pajamas.

"We got Kurt's license plate," I say. "I can send it to you."

"Do that." She clicks and unclicks her pen. "Just how close did you get to him?"

"We were careful."

"Promise me you won't go back there? These people are dangerous."

"OK . . ." I pace the room.

"We need to be extremely careful. It's delicate. If they get any hint of this, Devi or her family could be in danger, or they could move her on. We need to keep this very quiet. In other cases—"

"This has happened here before?" I sound like a huge baby – of course this has happened before.

"Afraid so. Look, leave it to us now. We know what we're doing." She pauses. "One more thing. We've been using a copy, but we need the original diary. Can you drop it into the station?"

I pace the other way. Of course it had been too easy. I had actually thought I could help without putting myself at risk at school again. But no such luck.

"OK," I say, my heart thundering now.

"Great. The sooner the better. Thanks again, Melati. I'll be in touch." She hangs up.

I throw my phone on my bed. What if I get sprung when I take the diary from Stokes again?

There are a couple of cars in the staff car park but no navy Subaru wagon.

Phew.

I pull my hoodie forward to hide my profile and adjust my backpack. Dressed in black I look like a burglar, apart from the netball I'm hugging to my side. If anyone asks I'm here to practise my shooting – not that I've played since Grade Five.

A large camellia tree makes an ideal hiding spot and I crouch behind it, my sneakers sinking into the soggy garden bed, and risk a peek through Stokes' window. There's the armchair, his desk, and his blank computer screen. A fleshy arm moves back and forth, then out of sight. I squat down so I'm under the window frame, grip the ledge, and push up on my toes until my nose reaches the window. A whistling woman rolls a vacuum cleaner over the marmalade-colored carpet. I duck down until the vacuum dies, then peek again. The woman dusts Stokes' bookshelf, stops and pulls out a book, turns up her nose, and slides the book back into place. She drags the vacuum out the door.

I edge around the building until I'm at the main door. Through a glass panel I can see the empty hallway and I tiptoe inside. The vacuum hums inside another office. I scoot down the stretch of thick carpet, reach Stokes' office, and pull the door shut behind me. After dumping my netball on the armchair I try the filing cabinet, but it's locked. The mints tin with the keys isn't in its usual spot behind the monitor. With fumbling fingers I search behind a jar of pens and under document trays and books, but I can't find the tin. The top drawer of his desk is locked too. Where are they?

In the second it takes me to realize I can't hear the vacuum anymore, there are footsteps outside his door. I dive under Stokes' desk and pull his chair close. I watch white-sneakered feet cross the floor, then stop in the middle of the room. My heart races when I spot my netball on the armchair.

I'm a goner.

The shoes pivot and stride toward the bookshelf.

Keep going, keep going.

She stops in front of the bookshelf, snatches a pink fluffy duster, and walks to the door, closing it behind her.

I count to ten, let myself breathe, then shove the chair away and leap up. I scan the room and notice a photo of a grinning Stokes and his mate, clutching their surfboards with a glistening ocean in the background. I pull it down for a closer look. Next to Stokes there's a small *warung* with a couple frying something in a wok. They look Indonesian. Why hadn't I noticed it before? Something shifts at the back of my mind, but I can't put the pieces together.

Get the key. Get the diary. Get out. Now.

When I return the photo I knock a small metal Buddha on the shelf and something clinks. Under it I find a set of keys. I race to the filing cabinet. The second key works and I wrench the cabinet drawer open. At the back under a stack of papers my fingers find the file. I slip the diary into my backpack.

I retrace my steps, checking I've left everything the way I found it. With my netball under my arm, I dart across the room and squash my ear against the door. The cleaner is vacuuming the hallway.

Damn.

After a minute the vacuum groans and whistles to a stop. There's a metallic sound, like a bunch of keys being shaken, then footsteps approaching the door. I squash myself behind the door as a key slides into the lock and turns. The door handle twists back and forth and I cringe, but then it stops. Footsteps retreat. Holding my breath, I wait behind the door and listen to the cleaner locking and testing the other doors.

It grows quiet. I gnaw my lip and wait until I'm sure she's gone. I grip the door handle and try to turn it, but it won't open. I whirl around and look for another escape route.

The window.

The cleaner is loading equipment into her car and I tap my fingers against the frame, waiting for her to finish. She slams the trunk, eases into the car and turns out of the car park. With one last look around the room, I turn the lock on the window and haul it open.

My leg's halfway through when I hear the beeps. They're faint but they're accelerating, like a heart monitor that's about to explode.

THIRTY-EIGHT

The security alarm is howling. I sprint until I can't hear it anymore and collapse at an empty tram shelter, lungs burning, the netball in my lap.

If they work out it was me, I'm screwed. Absolutely screwed.

A tram pulls up and I climb on, throwing myself into a seat. There's no way the school will know. They'll think the cleaner set off the alarm by accident when she left.

I keep telling myself that, and by the time I reach the city I almost believe it.

After I drop the diary off for Rose at the police station, I jump on the tram home. A young couple staggers on. They hang off each other and bump into an old Greek man with a shopping cart who's sitting near me. They giggle through their apologies, squeeze into a corner, and kiss. I try to check my phone but I can't concentrate with the sound of them. It's gross, but they're so natural about it.

I always thought Michael and I were just mates. But it crept up on me. When did being mates blend into this? I take my memories apart one by one. The wild, protective look on Michael's face when he found me with Kurt stabbing the EpiPen into my leg. Giving me the helmet when we were on the bike. Caring about Devi as much as I do. Sneaking out with Jack's car to help me. Listening to my woes from Year Nine. Running around graffiti-covered laneways together. Climbing Merapi, orange lights flaming in our eyes.

He deserves to know about Rose. My thumb hovers over his number on my phone.

It's dark outside and the fruit bats are fighting over the fig tree in the backyard. Rachel and I loll in front of the TV, bags of corn chips within easy reach, six episodes into our bingefest. Ivan sinks his fangs into a creamy neck and credits flash on to the screen. He's my favorite – he's funny and he looks like a Nordic supermodel. Who could ask for more?

With the Sri Lankans gone, Dad in East Timor, and Mum deep in a massage retreat, the house throbs with emptiness. Since I gave the diary to Rose, days have passed with no news from her and I've been obsessing about Devi. Worse still, I've been a total freak, hiding whenever someone knocks at the door, convinced that the police are going to haul me away for breaking into Stokes' office. Having Rachel stay is calming my jangled nerves.

She's also helping me stop messaging Michael. He's been camping at Wilson's Prom with his family and the reception was shit. In my weaker moments I wanted him to rush back to see me, but then I was the one who couldn't wait to run from his rooftop.

Tomorrow. I'll message him tomorrow.

Rachel is asleep on a beanbag, her breathing heavy. The TV paints the room with an eerie glow. I find my phone in an empty bag of chips and dust off the crumbs, but there's nothing from Rose. Why hasn't she called?

My phone shakes with a message. I sigh when I see it's from Mum.

"What? What is it?" Rachel rubs the sleep from her eyes and rolls off her beanbag.

I read Mum's text aloud: *Hi darling, the hinterlands were heavenly and hard to leave behind, but I missed you. See you in a few hours. Love Mum xxx. P.S. Hope you haven't trashed the house* 😉

"Trashed? Would this fit her definition?" Rachel says.

Cups of Indomie noodles with forks glued to the sides, empty bags of chips, grease-stained pizza boxes, a bottle of my favorite sambal lolling in front of the heater.

"Coffee?" I say.

Rachel nods.

The kitchen is foul. Piles of dishes, tangles of vegetable peelings, and noodles glued to the floor.

"Oh no." I shield my eyes with my hand and reach for the coffee machine.

Rachel finds the rubber gloves hanging over the sink and runs the hot water. I hug her.

An hour later the house looks like a home again instead of a crack den. I'm all fresh and minty from my shower. Rachel has gone home "to detox" before school begins tomorrow. At least it will be a short week. We have two student-free days while the teachers meet up for planning.

My phone rings. When I spot Rose's name on the caller ID my skin prickles.

"Look, Melati, we've had a translator check the diary," she says. "They essentially confirmed your translation."

"Great," I say.

"But we need to do a formal interview with you, today if possible. Can you make it?"

I freeze. "You want to interview me?"

Rose doesn't know about my police history and I fudged the detail about how I found the diary. I pull at the dry skin on my bottom lip.

"It's just procedure, we need things on the record."

"OK," I say, pulling the skin so hard it bleeds.

"Good. You need to have an adult with you. A parent or a guardian."

With Dad away it has to be Mum. How the hell am I going to explain this to her? Since The Year I Stuffed Up, Mum's seriously uptight about me and police stations. Today just gets better.

I rush into the police building on La Trobe Street and spot Mum. She's lost a bit of weight and her skin is dewy from all the righteous green smoothies they've pumped into her, but there are major frown lines across her forehead. Her post-retreat glow is already slipping thanks to me. I paste on my best fake smile.

"Hi Mum." I grab her for a hug.

She pulls away and grips my arms. "Why didn't you tell me what was going on?"

"Don't stress. I'm not in trouble, I'm helping the police—"

"I know, Agent Hanna explained it to me over the phone." She shakes her head. "But why didn't you answer my calls?"

A message was the easiest way to break the news to Mum about the interview. After I sent it I headed to the city and ate my death-row meal of fried pork dumplings. Because I knew once Mum found out what I'd been up to, today could be my last day of freedom – ever.

"Melati?" An Asian woman in her early thirties stands in front of us wearing a pin-striped suit. "I'm Agent Rose Hanna." Her long black ponytail shifts to one side when she holds out her hand. Her polished fingernails match her red shoes. When I shake her hand I try to hide my ragged nails.

"This is my Mum."

"Sylvie."

"Thanks so much for coming in at short notice. This way." Rose strides toward the security desk, her heels making sharp taps on the waxy floor. We collect passes, walk through a barrier gate and enter an elevator that is half-full of people in uniforms and plain clothes.

"We'll go up to the seventh floor."

I concentrate on the floor numbers on the panel above the door. Michael has a police interview today, too, but I'm not sure when. It felt good talking to him about all of this. Luckily his excitement about the police helped us avoid talking about other things.

Like kissing.

There's a uniformed cop next to me, who looks only about four years older than me. He's got short blond hair, dark circles under his eyes, and he's staring at me, big time. When I meet his eyes, his glance flickers away and settles on Rose's pinstriped butt.

Creep.

A robotic female voice announces "seventh floor" and Rose guides us out, past a sea of heads bent over desks, clusters of people talking to each other, and rooms with glass walls, drooping gray plastic blinds, and pale beige doors. She opens one of these doors and we step inside.

"Make yourselves comfortable, my colleague will be joining us in a moment." Rose sits down at the table.

I slide into a seat beside Mum. A uniformed cop enters, the fluorescent lights shining on his gelled, wavy black hair. "This is Agent Tony Caruso who is working with me on the case," Rose says.

Tony shakes our hands. He sits next to Rose and places a laptop and a large file on the table. He rolls his sleeves back. Something about him reminds me of the cop at Brunswick Police Station. It's their heavy-on-the-product hair, the shape of their eyes, and their muscly arms. They could almost be related.

My heart is racing. It's those lights, those awful eyeball-drying fluoro tubes on the ceiling. Calm down, keep it together for Devi.

"Thanks for your time today. We're keen to wrap this up as quickly as we can." Rose slides on red-framed glasses and opens an official-looking notebook. Tony starts recording and recites some details about the interview.

Out of the corner of my eye Mum shifts forward onto the edge of her chair.

Rose removes a plastic evidence bag from the file. The diary's inside it. "Melati, can you confirm that this is the diary you translated?"

"Yes," I say.

"How did you obtain it?" She pushes her glasses back up the bridge of her nose.

I swallow but I can't seem to get the dryness out of my throat. In my peripheral vision I can see Mum eyeballing me as I give them the facts.

"I felt bad about taking it and wanted to return it, but then I realized it was in Indonesian and that it wasn't Libby's diary, but Devi's."

"What did you find out about Devi?" Rose says.

"Her parents sent her to Melbourne to work as a nanny for a family." I take a breath. "But when she got here, her boss, this Kurt guy, forced her to work in his brothel. She's basically a slave. A prisoner." My voice cracks.

Tony taps away at the keyboard.

"Who did you tell when you found out about this?"

"Michael. Michael Quirke. He checked my translation, found the same thing."

"Our translator remarked on your accuracy." Rose gives me a half-smile. "Did you tell anyone else?"

"Just Yuliana—"

"Who?" Mum touches my arm.

"Devi's teacher, we tracked her down in Indonesia."

"Right, I've really got no idea what's going on in your life, have I?" Mum says.

"Anyone else?" Rose says.

"My best friend, Rachel."

"That's it?"

"I couldn't really tell anyone, I mean I was stuck because I'd taken the diary. But Michael told the police. Well, he tried."

Rose scribbles in her notebook and Tony reads over her shoulder, then types something. I watch Rose because I don't want to look in Mum's direction. Rose has high cheekbones and skin so smooth it looks polished. If she came to our school careers night everyone would be signing up to become police officers.

"How did you locate the brothel?"

"What? You're not serious?" Mum says.

"We were so worried about Devi and didn't know

what to do . . . We followed Stokes and he led us there."

"For the record, why do you think it's the right brothel?" Rose asks.

"We saw Stokes go down the lane and there was nowhere else for him to go. It fits Devi's description," I say. "And we saw Kurt, Devi's pimp there. He matches the drawing in her diary. I took his photo and Michael has his license plate number."

Mum's hands are gripping the edge of the table now.

Rose spreads blown-up versions of our photos across the table. "Interestingly, we got some results when we ran those plates. A taskforce has had their eye on Kurt for a while but up until now they couldn't pin anything on him. They're delighted you brought this to us."

I can't help smiling.

"So what's the taskforce going to do?" I ask.

Tony whispers something to Rose, then slips out of the room. She turns back to us.

"They're working with us. But you need to understand that if word gets out it could jeopardize the investigation and Devi's safety, even her life. It's common in cases like this that the pimps move the victims around. If that happens we could lose our chance to bust them and we might not be able to find her again."

We can't lose Devi, we're so close. We just can't.

THIRTY-NINE

In the interview room the fluoro lights buzz and snap overhead. Mum takes a deep breath. "There's one thing I'm having trouble with. Mr. Stokes must have Devi's diary because he's been exploiting her, a sixteen-year-old trafficking victim. He could even be part of it, the trafficking ring." She touches her throat. "That really concerns me. I mean, this man is the counselor at a girls' school. He's guiding my daughter and other young women and we don't know what he's involved in. Mel, you see him once a fortnight?"

"Once a week," I say.

Mum raises her hands. "I've got to talk to the school about this, it's completely unacceptable. They'd be horrified if they knew."

Rose considers her. "That's understandable. I think any

parent would have the same reaction. But we need to talk to him before we can draw any conclusions." She straightens her notebook. "I'll need you to delay talking to the school until we've had a chance to complete the investigation."

"How long will that take?"

"A few days. Max."

Mum purses her lips. "Can you avoid him when school goes back?"

"Sure, I've been doing it for weeks," I say.

Tony strides back into the room and hands me my statement. "Give it a good read, and if you're happy sign at the bottom."

Mum and I study the statement. I sign, struggling to keep my signature on the line.

Rose thanks us. "Tony and I were saying before that we see a lot of teenagers in our work, usually for the wrong reasons. So it's nice to meet a young person who is trying to do the right thing. I know your mother is worried because you've taken risks. While I'd urge you not to take things into your own hands in future, you should feel proud of how you've helped us."

I try not to think of another interview with another cop and how Mum's face was sick with shame.

Outside the police building, Mum asks if I want a coffee

but doesn't wait for my answer. She strides toward the nearest café. I dawdle behind her. This is going to be interrogation number two. Will she be calmer in public? I cross my fingers inside the pocket of my hoodie and follow her into the café.

My eyes widen. Michael and his dad are sitting in an empty corner of the café, away from all the cops and suits. I wave at him and tell Mum. His face brightens and something roars in my chest. I've been an idiot.

When we reach their table, Mr. Quirke jumps up to shake Mum's hand and to shift their stack of plates and cups to a neighboring table.

"Big lunch?" Mum asks.

"Police interviews and camping seem to make Michael hungry. But I suspect it was all a ploy so he didn't have to answer my questions."

They laugh but Michael rolls his eyes.

My knee brushes Michael's as I sit down and I jerk it away.

"We've just had our interview," Mum says, glancing at me.

"How did it go?" Mr. Quirke says.

"Dad, we can't talk about it." Michael shifts in his chair.

A waiter arrives with our drinks.

Mr. Quirke turns to Mum. "Michael tells me you

lived in Bandung for a while? We've got some relatives there but most of them are in Jogja now."

"That's right, when Mel was little. Not that she can remember."

"I do," I say. "Some of it anyway."

"She's tried to keep up her Indonesian ever since. And her grandmother, my mother-in-law, was Indonesian."

"I tried to make sure Michael and the boys didn't lose theirs, but they didn't want to go near it for a while." He lowers his voice. "After their mother died the other two just wanted to forget."

Michael studies the bottom of his coffee cup like he's found a hidden world there. Mum rubs her hand over her mouth and I can tell she's dying to know more, but it's too awkward to ask.

"So this Devi, she's from Salatiga?" Mr. Quirke says.

"Just near there. And near Pineapple Village." I sip my hot chocolate.

"Really?"

"That's what I mean, Dad. I had to help her," Michael says.

"You've got a connection to the area?" Mum says.

Mr. Quirke lowers his glass. "My late wife was from a village nearby. I studied Indonesian at university there and did a homestay with her family, that's how we met. We even married in Salatiga."

"Sounds romantic."

"They're a lovely family. Homestays were a lifeline for them, they were really struggling back then. I'm pretty sure my wife's family didn't eat some of the time so they could feed the greedy Australian boy." He smiles.

"Did your wife finish school?" I ask.

"They pulled her out of school at fifteen to work in a hotel. But she finished her education in Australia, after we married. Said it was her second chance."

"Mum was lucky she met Dad," Michael says.

"I've never heard you call it lucky before." Mr. Quirke laughs.

"Devi's diary made me think," Michael says.

I had no idea that Michael felt a connection to Devi through his mum. But then how much do I really know about him? Most of the time I've spent with him I've been preoccupied with helping Devi, not hearing his life story.

"On balance, I'm proud of you." Mr. Quirke raises his chin. "But I know you took Jack's car—"

"Dad—" Michael edges forward in his chair.

"I recognized the dashboard in the photo."

"Jack would've let me, I'm a good driver."

"Really, Michael? You're going to argue about this?"

Michael slides back down in his chair and crosses his arms.

"Why didn't you ask me for help? Maybe we could've found another way."

I'm squirming inside, watching Michael in the headlights.

"It's my fault, Mr. Quirke. I begged Michael to help. We hadn't found the brothel then, all we had was the diary. I didn't want to tell anyone because I didn't want Stokes to know I stole the diary – I'd be in so much trouble at school."

They might still expel me.

There's a hint of a smile on Mr. Quirke's face. "You're a loyal friend, Melati."

"Michael's the loyal one. He didn't have to do any of this but he went out of his way."

Mr. Quirke ruffles Michael's hair. "He's a good lad."

"I'm still reeling." Mum shakes her head. "I'm so glad that you helped Mel. I hate to think of her doing this on her own."

Mum's less stressed out than I thought she'd be. Maybe The Year I Stuffed Up toughened her.

"You've taken huge risks. Again. But at least it's not for a stupid volcano this time."

"Volcano?" Mr. Quirke looks at Mum, then at me and Michael.

"Uh, yeah." Michael says.

"Why don't you fill me in?"

While Mr. Quirke gives Michael the third degree, Mum shifts her chair closer to mine.

"Stealing from the school counselor, stalking him, getting into a car with an unlicensed driver." She checks each item off on her fingers. "I don't know what to do with you, it's like you think you're bulletproof. You did so well last year." Her voice is tight. "How could you mess with criminals like that? Why didn't you tell me?"

"You'd freak." I rotate my cup on its saucer. "Like you are now."

She pretends she hasn't heard me. "When I think of the people involved . . . These people are animals and if they worked out what you were doing . . . Did you at least talk to your dad?"

"He was preoccupied." My cup wobbles and I grab it just in time. "We weren't stupid."

"I'm horrified about the risks you've taken." Mum shoves a strand of hair behind her ear. "But overall I'm really proud of you. It's amazing what you've done. Everything the police said. How you've helped them. And your concern for that girl . . ."

She's proud of me. *Proud* of me. When did I last feel that? I'm so overwhelmed I don't notice her silence for a moment. "What, Mum?"

"I've been hard on you, but I was so worried. Some of the things I said – I probably made you feel pretty bad about yourself." She presses her hands against the table. "But you can stop trying to make up for Year Nine now. It's OK."

There's a sudden lightness in my chest. It takes me a moment to realize it's where shame used to live.

Since the police interview I've been wired, waiting for news, but I've heard nothing. Rose said they'd keep us informed, but does that mean they'll only contact us when it's all over? Last night Mum found me prowling around the house at one in the morning and convinced me to swallow her Chinese medicine cure for insomnia.

I nearly gagged, but it worked.

It's actually nice having her around.

Things are better with Michael, but we haven't hung out. We need to talk but I cringe every time I think about it, even though I miss him heaps. Can't we work it out telepathically?

Yeah, good plan.

This morning I couldn't find my hat, so I use the back gate at school near the staff car park to avoid the evil prefects out the front. The path winds by the garden and I wander into a cloud of rich scent from a cluster of roses. A movement to my left catches my eye. It's Stokes at his office window, shielding his eyes against the morning glare, his head turned in my direction. Out of habit I wave to him, but there's a deep ridge across his brow and his mouth is tight. He gives me a single wave and steps away.

Something cold lodges in my throat. The roses are too sweet now, their scent is all over me. Questions shoot at me like poison arrows.

Does Stokes know I've been in his office?

If he does, what's he going to do about it?

By the time I slide into my seat beside Rachel in double math I'm convinced I'm screwed. Stokes knows and he's going to report me. Hello expulsion. He's never given me a hard look like that before.

"What's up with you?" Rachel says.

"What?" I pull out my books.

"You're all blotchy and pink."

I touch my cheeks and they're warm and my skin is prickly.

Ms. Monk writes a long series of equations on the board and I try to lose myself in the numbers, anything to block the questions that keep forming. Like, have the police contacted Stokes yet? Stokes' look – full of suspicion and hurt – keeps repeating on me, and for some reason I feel guilty.

But why should I care? The man's a creep.

Ms. Monk's writing blurs into hieroglyphics when it hits me: I have to talk to Stokes before the police do. He might understand if I reach him first, then he might not snitch on me. I've got an appointment with him in a few days but I could see him at recess instead. I picture myself in his cane armchair, pouring everything out, Stokes steepling his hands as he listens to me, nodding when it all begins to make sense.

Yeah, right.

At recess I make an excuse and dodge Rache. I'm on a mission to talk to Stokes. I dash through the yard, but near the staff room I freeze mid-stride.

I would recognize that ponytail anywhere – long, black, and soft, swinging from side to side like a pendulum. Beside her, a man with gelled dark hair and broad shoulders. A secretary is walking with them, guiding Rose and Tony in the direction of Stokes' office.

My alarm wakes me early. I'm deep under when it screeches at me, but I spring out of bed, determined to deal with Stokes before the stress drives me crazy. I can't last another day without talking to him.

When I reach school the place is deserted and Stokes' door is closed. I wonder if I'm too early, but I knock anyway.

"Come in," he says, and I jump out of my skin.

I ease the door open.

Stokes starts when he sees me. "Mel, you look exhausted. Come in." He stands up, strides to the door and closes it behind me.

I perch on the edge of the armchair.

"So what's up?" He sounds casual but there's an edge to his voice. "You're a day early."

"What? Oh." He's talking about our appointment. "I wanted to catch you earlier."

He raises an eyebrow, then grabs his tablet from his desk and checks something on it. "You've missed two appointments, that's riding pretty close to the wind."

"Sorry about that."

I study him. Before I thought he was so together. So Zen. But when it comes to his own stuff he's as messed up as the rest of us.

Stokes lowers his tablet to his desk. "It was you, wasn't it?"

FORTY

Stokes has thrown a bucket of ice water in my face and it stings, even though I knew it was coming.

"The diary? Yeah, I took it." I want to break eye contact, but I don't. Something about his look softens a bit, or maybe I'm imagining it. "I'm sorry, I shouldn't have looked in your filing cabinet. It was unlocked and I was really pissed off with Libby and I wanted to clear my name so I went looking for her file and," I take a deep breath, "one thing led to another."

Stokes nods. "I know, the police told me. And security said there might have been a break-in. The only thing missing was the diary." He pins me with his eyes. "That was you too, wasn't it?"

I nod and hang my head. This is all wrong, why am I feeling guilty when he's the one visiting trafficked women? I try to superimpose a creep mask on to his face, but it won't stick.

"The police needed it," I say. "It was the only way."

"No, it wasn't." He glares at me. "Why didn't you come to me? If I'd known I never would have . . ." He shakes his head. "I had no idea what was in the diary."

"What do you mean?" I screw up my face.

"You could have come to me, told me what you'd found. I tried to translate it but I've got five words of Indonesian and online sites are hopeless. When the police told me I was horrified."

"But you knew something was up, you were seeing Devi. You must have known."

Stokes' eyes widen. "Wow, you don't think much of me, do you?" He shakes his head. "I never saw Devi. I only saw one woman there, someone older, Mariska."

"Was she trafficked too?"

He shakes his head.

"But how do you know?"

"Well, you can tell. She wasn't scared. If anything, at times she scared me. She's fierce."

I cringe. "That doesn't mean she wasn't, does it? I mean, how can you be sure? From what Devi said in her diary Kurt forced her to act like she was enjoying it, or he'd hurt her."

My chest feels tight and I look away from him. Maybe I'm being too much of a hard-ass.

"When the police told me . . ." His voice cracks. "I'm devastated, it's horrific. To think what she's going through. To think I went to that place. You've got to believe me, I would never, ever have gone there if I'd had any suspicion they trafficked women. I'm not a monster, Mel. You know that."

His eyes are bright, almost pleading, but I look away.

"Going to a brothel isn't illegal," he says.

But breaking in is. He doesn't have to say it.

My heart wobbles when I meet his eyes. That hard look is back and his mouth is tight. But now I notice the shadows under his eyes. This is my one chance to ask him all the questions that have kept me awake at night.

"If you weren't seeing Devi, how did you get her diary?"

"Have you ever thought of a career in policing?" Stokes shakes his head. "I did meet Devi in passing, twice. Tried out my five words of Indonesian on her, made her laugh."

"But how did you get it?"

"I first noticed it in my sports bag after the second time I met her. Devi had been sitting near me in the guest lounge. She must have slipped it in there – that's all I can think of. I have no idea how, or why."

I rub my forehead. "Didn't you ask her?"

"I tried. I went back several times to speak to her but she was never available." He squeezes his hands together. "I didn't know what to do and I didn't have the diary very long before it went missing." He edges back in his chair and rolls into a nest of cardboard boxes tucked under his desk.

Packing boxes.

"Are you leaving?"

Stokes sighs. "Yeah. I wanted to leave immediately but Sturgeon wasn't happy, reminded me of my contract, the notice I've got to give." He takes a deep breath. "So I told her . . . what she needed to know."

My heart skitters. I want to ask if he told her about me, but he's frowning at me already. "Why would you do that?" I ask.

He sags in his chair. "Because as soon as the police knocked on my door I knew I was finished here. It'll get out. Things do in this place."

"It doesn't have to. You don't have to quit."

"Mel, I can't trust you. You had your reasons, I know." He holds my gaze for a long moment. "But you've gone through my things, stolen from me, broken into my office, and followed me."

When he says it like that I sound like a total psycho.

"You could have just talked to me," he says.

"You've got to be kidding? There was no way."

Why do I feel like the bad guy again? Am I really a shit or is he a master manipulator?

"What about your wife? Does she know?"

Stokes wiggles his ring finger. "You mean this? This isn't real. I've never been married."

"Huh?" I screw up my face.

"No way. I'd never sign up for that patriarchal institution."

"But you go to brothels?" My cheeks burn, I hadn't meant to say that out loud. Or had I?

"Wow," Stokes says.

I pull at the neck of my shirt.

"One brothel, I've been to one. Ever. And I'm not going again, not after what's happened."

I still don't get it, why would Stokes go in the first place? But that's a question I can't seem to ask.

"I'm not proud of it, but I'm not ashamed, if that's what you want from me."

It seems like neither of us can admit we're sorry.

"If you're not married why do you wear the ring?"

"I should take it off. Ms. Krantz gave me the idea, actually. Said I should wear it because I'm a thirty-two-year-old male at a girls' school. It made sense."

"You're single?"

Stokes stares at me but it's like he's not looking at me at all. He's turning something over in his mind.

"I did have a partner but we broke up last year. She was preg—" He stops himself. "I never thought I'd be in this position."

His eyes are shiny. Please don't cry, I can't handle it. This is all wrong. Only students are meant to cry in this room.

"You'd better leave." His voice cracks.

I walk out of the door in a daze. This wasn't how it was meant to happen. I was so clear before: Stokes was a creep, let him have it. Now my conscience is burning with all those memories of the other Stokes. The Stokes who understood me without letting me off the hook or ever judging me.

Why do I feel like I've failed him?

I've got a free period in the afternoon, so I leave early. I wanted to hang out with Rachel but she has media. It's probably a good thing anyway. If I spend time with her I'll be tempted to rant about Stokes. That's the last thing we need.

A tram rolls up and I jump on. Chis shrinks behind me. Things have changed so much in just a few days – the police, Mum, Stokes. I stretch out my legs and try not to think about how much the Surgeon knows, and what she'll do about it. All I can do is wait and see.

But nothing's changed for Devi.

My phone buzzes with a new text.

Michael: *Any news?*

Me: *Nope* ☹ *will let you know.*

Michael: ☺

When I reach home, Mum's in the kitchen poring over an article.

"Want some tea?" I say.

"That'd be nice."

I turn the kettle on. "Stokes is leaving. Says he told Mrs. Sturgeon everything."

She looks up from the paper. "Well, that's that then."

I pour the hot water. "So you don't need to talk to the school any more."

"Guess not." She pretends to read again.

I pass her a mug and hover by the table.

"How did you find out?" Mum turns a page.

"I spoke to him."

"What?" Her eyebrows shoot up.

"Yeah. It was weird, not like I thought it would be at all."

She pushes the paper aside. "What do you mean?"

I flop into a chair. "Everything I thought was wrong."

I take a sip and it's scalding, but something about the hot wash of tea is comforting, like it's stopping my emotions from rising. I tell her what I found out. "I don't get it, Mum. He volunteers at soup kitchens and homework clubs but he went to the brothel. How can that be the same person?"

"I don't know, darling," Mum says. "I mean I thought maybe he was involved in trafficking and was exploiting that poor girl. So I'm relieved about that."

"Understatement of the year." I yank my teabag out of my mug and dump it on the saucer.

"If he's telling the truth," she says.

"You don't think . . ."

She shrugs. Mum used to give me certainty. Now she shares what she really thinks, not the stuff she thinks a parent should say. She's not protecting me from the gray bits of life anymore. I'm not sure I like it.

"You were there. Did you believe him?" Mum says. "What's your gut tell you?"

I remember the sharp, hurt look in his eyes. "That he was telling the truth."

"Then I bet you're right. But I don't understand how anyone could go to a brothel and ignore the possibility that women, *girls*, might be there against their will." She grips her mug. "I can be a bit judgemental though –"

I fake cough.

"Yeah, I'm sure you've never noticed." She twists her mouth.

"How do you know if someone's a good person or not, Mum?"

She shrugs and puts her mug down. "I guess you look at the sum of the person. But it can take a long time to know someone that well."

It hurts to look at myself. I felt like the criminal when Stokes told me all of the ways I'd betrayed him. Everything I'd done had been to help Devi, but for Stokes it didn't stack up.

"The worst was when he told me about his break-up with his girlfriend. He was about to cry. I didn't know what to do, it would have felt wrong to comfort him when I'd been accusing him of all this stuff." I suck in a breath. "Then he told me to leave and I felt like shit."

Mum rests her hand on my back. "That's tough. When he calms down he'll understand, he knows you well."

"I know what it's like to feel . . ."

"Judged?"

"Like you've disappointed people." I sigh. "But if men didn't go to sex workers this never would have happened to Devi."

She nods. "Have you heard from Rose?"

"No, and it's driving me crazy."

"You'll hear something soon."

She strokes my hair back from my face, and for once I let her.

My phone is ringing. I jerk awake and breathe in a mouthful of fur. Hedy is swishing her tail in my face. I shove her out of the way. A Scandinavian crime drama is flickering on TV, my half-eaten toasted sandwich is on the coffee table and the house is now dark. My phone is on the floor and I scramble to answer it before it rings out.

It's Rose.

"Melati," Rose says immediately. "We found Devi."

"Yes!" I punch the air. Then I freeze. "Is she safe?"

"Yes, we got her out."

"Thank you, thank you, thank you." I whoop and dance around the couch and a freaked-out Hedy dodges my feet.

Rose continues. "The raid was a big success. Everyone's safe—"

"What do you mean everyone?"

"There were seven other victims. But they're all safe now. They're being looked after."

Eight women. I'd been so focused on Devi I'd forgotten there could be others.

"I can't say much because we're preparing our case, but it all went really well. We'll be taking statements from all the women and you might need to give evidence down the track—"

"What? In court?" I start pacing.

"It's possible. But these cases take a long time. It could be a year before it's heard."

"A year?" My voice rises.

"Maybe less, maybe more."

A year before Devi has any chance of justice. A year she'll spend agonizing and waiting for the court case. Devi is free, but this isn't over for her.

"Can I contact her?"

"We'll see, but it's up to Devi."

We say goodbye. Devi is free, she's safe.

I can't get through to Michael so I leave a message, then melt into my bed.

FORTY-ONE

Ping! Ping! Ping!

I clamp a pillow over my head but the noise is stubborn. I tunnel out from under my comforter and look out the window. Michael's outside, his hand clutching another pebble. I can't stop my smile. His face tells me everything I need to know. His dad's dog, Darius, is by his side in a ridiculous orange dog jacket. I wrench the window open and the air chills me.

"Rapunzel!" Michael yells.

"Ha, ha." My eyes are bleary with sleep. "What time is it?"

"Ten."

"Shit. Hang on." I scramble to the bathroom, throw cold water on my face, fight with my hair, douse myself with body spray, and jump into cargos and a hoodie. My eyes are puffy and I look like a marsupial. I tip my room upside down until I find my sunglasses and shove them on.

I race downstairs, tell Mum I'm going out. When I see Michael my words get tangled in my throat. Darius heads straight for my crotch, but I divert him by tickling his ears and neck. He wedges his head against my knees and I start to giggle.

"Sit!" Michael says.

Darius ignores him and strains against my legs.

"Sit, Darius!" Michael rolls his eyes. "Hey, I got your message." He shows me his phone. "Did you see the story in the *Tribune*?"

"Really?" I grab his phone. "But it's just one line."

"Guess they'll put up a bigger story later." Michael punches my arm, his eyes shining. "Why aren't you more excited?"

"I am, I am. It's great, it's . . ." I pass his phone back. "It's Devi. Now she's out, I can't help thinking . . ."

"Yeah, but you can still enjoy it. You deserve it."

"So do you." I magnify the article and something about the starkness of the story on the screen hits me. "She's out, she's really out!"

Darius tugs us all the way to CERES, the permaculture farm down the street. He romps with the other dogs, then sprawls at our feet to warm his butt in the winter sun. We sit by the edge of the café crowd and slurp hot chocolates. Michael grabs an abandoned copy of the *Tribune* from a nearby table and we leaf through it.

"Nup, nothing here." Michael folds up the paper, stretches back in the sun. I try to look away from the strip of exposed flesh above his jeans.

"So where were you last night?" I say.

"Working at Petro's."

"Oh yeah, I totally forgot about that."

Michael works at this grimy kebab caravan on High Street. They pay crappy rates, cash in hand, but he does it for the free food.

"They're really uptight about us using our phones, so by the time I heard your message it was late. I thought of coming round . . ."

"You did?"

He swings upright and scratches Darius under the collar. "It seemed like I should be with you."

Gentle wings flutter in my chest and our eyes meet.

"But I smelt like chip fat. Garlic sauce. Chicken salt. Not good."

He doesn't want to smell gross around me.

"You know, it's really good to see you," I say.

"Yeah." His smile is almost shy.

Looking at him now, the sun shining on his face, my heart thrumming, the weirdness has melted away. The sun warms the top of my head and I tilt my chair back until the rays hit my cheeks. But my happiness tilts when I think of Devi.

Michael asks what will happen to her and I share what Rose told me.

"It depends if she wants to testify against them. If it were me I'd want to get the hell out of here."

"Every now and again it hits me, you know? What they did to her. I always knew, but sometimes it goes deep into my bones, this sick, horrible feeling." He pulls at his jacket. "Do you ever wonder about her parents? If they knew? If they sold her?"

"No way. They wouldn't . . . "

He shrugs and looks away. "I wonder. It happens, you know. I've done some research."

"There was no hint of that in her diary."

"Maybe she didn't know."

The dog places his muzzle on Michael's thigh and stares up at him.

"Darius, you're alright, you know." He rubs the dog's head.

A fluffed-up Maltese approaches and lures Darius away. Michael smirks for a second, before his mouth turns down. "They should bring back medieval punishments for these guys."

"Yeah, hung, drawn, and quartered. I'd be happy with that."

We're in the backyard, sneaking two of Dad's beers to celebrate Devi's freedom.

"Do you ever think about Kurt?"

"Sometimes." Michael rips the label from his bottle. "He's in jail, isn't he?"

"Yeah, but what if he gets bail?"

He swings his chair upright. "Shit, I didn't even think about it."

"Kurt saw our faces."

"But he doesn't know we're involved. Even if he did, there's no way he could track us down. The police told me and Dad they'd protect our identities."

"I guess." Thinking about Kurt makes me jittery. I take another swig and wipe beer foam off my top lip.

The autumn sun is fading and the cold drives us indoors. When Darius' paws hit the kitchen floor, Hedy scrams and goes into deep cover. Michael has decided to hang and watch the evening news with me. We're hoping for more of a story. Mum's left money because she's gone to a function so we order pizza and sprawl on the couch. He's well into his second beer but I'm still on my first. Alcohol and I have an uneasy truce at the moment.

But I can handle beer. I take another sip.

The Channel Seven news commences and we're on the edge of the couch, but our eyes glaze over when it's a story about another political battle in Canberra. I roll back into my corner of the couch. But a minute later we're on the edge of the couch again.

"Police have uncovered a sex-trafficking ring in Melbourne . . ." There's a night-time shot of the brothel, the neon lighting giving the laneway a chilling blue tint. The footage switches to Inspector Nolan, standing outside the police headquarters.

"Following the successful raid last night a number of suspects are now in custody. They've been charged with multiple offences, including trafficking and slavery. The victims are receiving medical attention and support. They're currently assisting with our investigation. This is a reminder that the heinous crime of sex trafficking can happen in Victoria."

The news switches to a story about footballers fighting in a nightclub. We break into wide smiles.

I'm heavy with all the pizza and beer but I'm buzzing and I can't stop bouncing around. Michael goes to leave and I want to say something meaningful. Trouble is I don't do meaningful. So I reach up and hug him. He hugs me back.

My face is against his jacket and he smells of beer and pine and warmth. We wrap around each other. I stretch on my tiptoes toward him, and then we're kissing. No teeth this time. It's electric and magic and just like it's meant to be. We stumble against the door, our bodies crushing together, his hands buried in my hair.

"I better go," Michael says eventually, a huge smile plastered across his face.

"You better."

With an equally goofy grin on my face, I push him through the door. He snaps on Darius' leash and the dog tugs him toward the darkness.

I lean against the doorframe for a while, a pulse beating in my neck. My legs are unsteady and I trip over the straggly line of empties in the kitchen. A bottle rolls across the floor but I ignore it. I find the couch and sit down, but feel no closer to the ground.

Whatever just happened between us, it better happen again.

FORTY-TWO

On Monday it's weird passing through the school gates and slipping into the school routine. Something huge has happened, but no one here knows.

After biology I head outside. The sun has punched a hole through the gray winter. In the distance Grace Vincent gives me a quick wave. It's the first time she's acknowledged me since the fight with Libby. Things might have been different if she'd stuck up for me, but then I might never have ended up in Stokes' office and stolen the diary. Devi might still be trapped. Maybe life has a twisted logic after all.

I head to the timber fort in the middle of the playground. When I reach it I notice Libby sitting with Marnie on the bench at the base of the fort. They used to sit there a bit, before all the shit went down. Libby manages to sneer at me and still keep talking. I make a point of yawning.

Rache is lounging at the top in the weak sun, nibbling a wrap.

"God, why are they sitting there?" I ask.

"They were there when I got here. But who cares?"

"Yeah, I guess. I've got to stop letting her get to me. Where are the others?" I ask.

"In the library, working on a group assignment for politics."

"That sucks." I sit down and unwrap a leftover pizza slice. Melted together mushrooms, olives, and mozzarella take me back to last night. Michael, beer, pizza, and kisses. Kisses that make me feel floaty, even today.

"What are you smiling about?" Rache swings upright.

"Nothing." My smile grows wider thinking of Michael, and of Devi.

"It's not nothing. Tell me." She locks eyes with me.

I keep chewing, watching Rache's impatience build.

She squeezes my shoulders with both hands. "What is it? You're killing me."

I put my pizza down. "I'm not sure you really want to hear about this . . . last time you didn't want to know."

Rachel examines me. "You're buzzing so much it's got to be good. I promise not to throw anything at you."

"You can't tell anyone about this, OK? No one. The cops said it could put me in danger."

She nods, crosses her heart.

"The police raided the brothel on Saturday night. They got Devi and some other women out. She's safe."

"Saturday. You dirty slut! Why didn't you tell me then?" Rachel trips over her words.

"Are you kidding? You didn't want to know," I say.

She ignores what I've just said. "Melati, you fucking hero! This is huge. But what happened? I need to know everything!"

I start to tell her. She makes me backtrack constantly to give her more detail, and I show her the Channel Seven footage.

"Mum is going to lap this up. She'll want to adopt you now."

I snort. "But you can't tell her, I'm serious."

"OK, I won't." Rachel rolls her plastic wrap into a ball and aims for the bin. She misses and hits Marnie on the head. "Shit! Sorry Marnie. Didn't mean to."

They shoot us death glares.

Rachel's eyes dance. "So what's happening with Michael?"

Something hits my temple. An apple core rolls toward the center of the platform. We stare at it like it's a hand grenade. Rachel's nostrils flare. I shake my head in warning.

"Sorry Gelati! Missed the bin," Libby says.

Rachel yells over the side of the fort before I can stop her. "Bin's the other way, loser."

I grab Rachel's blazer and tug her back. "This is what she wants, I'm still on probation."

Rachel shakes her head.

"Worthless skank. You should've been expelled." Libby's scowling up at me.

I roll my eyes. She can't reach me up here, and after everything that's happened I barely give a shit what she thinks. It's like a fly buzzing around at a picnic. Just a bit annoying.

"I used to think she was a bitch, but now I think she's a bit . . ." Rache taps her temple.

"Thinks she's Melati the fucking hero now," Libby shouts.

Hero?

"She must have been listening," Rache says.

When the bell sounds its first ring we jump to our feet and gather our things. I swing my leg over the top beam of the fort, but then I hesitate. Libby's at the base, her eyes flinty. Marnie's on the edge of the bench seat, watching Libby.

"No wonder you found that massage parlour, I mean brothel. Your mum probably works there," Libby yells.

Heat flares in my chest and I grip the wooden beam. "She's a masseuse, you idiot."

"Yeah, right," Libby says, turning away.

"At least my mum didn't dump me," I snap.

For a second the world stops spinning. Rachel freezes on the beam above mine. Libby has her back to us. Marnie tugs at her arm, but Libby doesn't budge. I hold my breath, until she steps away from us, her shoulders rising.

"Thought it was Armageddon time," Rachel says.

"Let's go," I say, the sting of her insult still coursing through me. How dare she have a go at Mum.

The second bell sounds and I start to climb down.

"Watch out!" Rachel yells, just as a shove against my side knocks me.

I grab the beam above me and get my balance, but then I slip and lose my footing again. I reach out, grasping air. The tree and fort tip sideways and I smash to the ground.

FORTY-THREE

I'm a kid at the beach again, knocked out by a huge dumping wave I didn't see coming.

"Mel. Oh, my God. I didn't mean to. Let me help you." A giant Libby looms over me, her voice shaking, reaching for my arms.

"Get away from her!" Rachel shoves her and crouches down beside me. "Un-fucking-believable. Are you alright?"

I squint and blink but I can't block out the dancing lights. A scrum of faces looks down at me. I try to move, but my legs are tangled beneath me. Rachel helps me shift into a sitting position.

"Can you get up?" she says.

With Rachel's arm under mine, I push off on my left leg and I'm up, but my right leg feels disconnected from my body. I ease my weight on to my right foot but the pain ricochets up my leg and a rush of nausea sweeps me off my feet.

Thanks to the hardcore drugs I'm on, one minute I'm alert, the next fuzziness rains down and I wake with a jerk half an hour later. It's been three days since I broke my leg and scored a Grade 2 concussion. Dr. Hoang ordered me to rest at home for at least two weeks. There's blue plaster covering my right leg from knee to ankle.

Mum pushes the living room door open with her shoulder, balancing a tray of soup and toast.

"You're awake," she says.

"Yeah, but I could pass out at any moment." I push back into the nest of pillows she's piled up for me on the couch.

"You've got to expect that." Mum sits down next to me and hands me the tray.

Her mother-of-the-year act is both comforting and weird, but it's good to be home. I was in hospital for one night and have the bleariest impressions of Xrays, wheelchairs and injections, but my memory of wanting to get the hell out of there is sharp.

"You know all this happened because I defended your honor?" I grab the spoon.

"So I heard." She smiles and smooths my hair back from my face.

"No one talks shit about my family." I slurp down some minestrone. "Except me."

The soup soothes my raggedy throat and warms my body. When I try to shift my leg the pain engulfs me. I brace myself and Mum shoots out a hand and holds my arm. It fades to a throb.

"The principal rang. Again." Mum adjusts my comforter.

I swallow my soup the wrong way and splutter.

"Don't worry, it's good news. Your probation is officially over and I've applied to have the warnings on your record removed. So we'll see."

"Seriously?"

"One hundred per cent. And they've suspended Libby while they investigate."

I never thought that would happen. Libby had gotten away with everything for so long. After all the pressure of this year, I feel dizzy.

"Mrs. Sturgeon was very nice actually, very caring. She was apologetic, but asked for our discretion about Stokes, said he'd been under a lot of stress. I think she's terrified we'll sue the school."

"How much would we get?"

Mum laughs for a moment, then presses her hands against her legs. "There's more. Mrs. Sturgeon wants to speak to you. She wants your version of events. And she didn't say as much, but she wants to know what you think should happen. To Libby."

"Do you think they'll expel her?" I drop the spoon and it clinks against the bowl.

"She wasn't specific, but they must be considering it."

Memories of the circle meeting and the Hartnetts' threat to lay charges against me return. The old anger pumps through my veins. But they didn't charge me and I got another chance. I sag against the pillows.

"You don't have to call her yet."

When I remember how I taunted Libby about her mum, my skin feels cold.

"What do you think I should do?"

"This one's for you, Mel." She picks up the tray.

I sigh. "But what do you think?"

"All I would say is that the girl is obviously troubled. But I can't tell you what to do."

"Since when?"

"Not anymore." She winks at me and leaves the room.

When we were searching for Devi I imagined that once she was safe I'd feel free and life would go back to normal. But nightmares haunt me. I'm in front of a locked dungeon door and Devi is on the other side. Through the keyhole I spy her trying to unlock the door with a gargantuan set of keys, but the keys multiply endlessly in her hands and she can't find the right one. I pound on the door, kick it and slam my body against it, but I can't open it.

When I wake, heart racing, back sticky with sweat, I tell myself she's safe, that it's the drugs messing with me, but something won't let me believe it. We've never met, never spoken. After weeks of being so close to her thoughts, now it's like she doesn't exist. Maybe if I hear from her the nightmares will stop.

It's Friday afternoon and Rachel has dropped by. She's painted my toenails blue to match my Smurf cast and laid out my survival pack across the couch: jumbo-sized corn chips, jam donuts, and a king-size block of chocolate. At the bottom of the heap I find a lonely packet of prunes and hold them up by one corner.

"What's this?"

"Mum put those in. Said the painkillers will be an absolute bitch for constipation and thought you might need some help."

"Can't wait." I drop the packet and return my gaze to the TV.

Hitchcock's *Rear Window* is on the screen. Rachel picked it out because she has to watch it for media studies. James Stewart sits in a wheelchair, his broken leg in a cast. A murderer's heavy footsteps climb the stairs to his apartment. Trapped, Stewart searches for a weapon.

I grab my phone. There's nothing from Rose. If Kurt made bail he'd be free to track me down. Thanks, Rache, for feeding my paranoia.

I text Rose: *Anything?*

"Hey, what about Libby?" Rache grins.

"Can't believe it."

Yesterday in between drug-induced naps and nightmares about Devi I thought about what to say to the Surgeon. When my leg hurts and I'm sick of my cast I want to hit Libby with a big dose of karma. But if she gets expelled will she just go to another school and do the same shit? None of the suspensions or threats changed anything for me – they just made me better at hiding.

Something else is niggling at me. Maybe I'm an idiot, but I remember Libby's face after my fall. There was real concern. She wasn't faking it.

"You saw more than me. What actually happened with Libby?"

"Well, she shoved you hard and you fell." Rachel whistles and sketches the arc of my fall in the air.

"Do you think she meant for me to fall?"

"It happened fast. Maybe she didn't mean for you to go down like that, but I'm not sure."

I nibble at a square of chocolate.

"What are you going to say to the Surgeon?" Rachel says.

I shrug. "Don't know."

Her eyes linger on me. "Did you hear that Stokes is working at St Michael's College?"

"So it's official?"

"You knew?"

I spill about my last encounter with Stokes.

"Do you believe him, that he didn't see Devi?"

"Pretty much. He was really upset."

"One of the Year Twelves saw him at the pub over a week ago. Said he was so drunk and down she barely recognized him." She frowns. "Why didn't you tell me about this before?"

There's been so much I haven't told her over the last two months.

Scratch that. Since I met her.

"Rache, there's some stuff you don't know about me."

And I tell her.

Everything.

FORTY-FOUR

When I reach the kitchen I collapse against the island bench with my crutches and pant. Dishes are piled around the sink and steam escapes from a cast-iron casserole dish on the stove. The rich scents of lemongrass, lamb, and spices mix with the sweetness of toasted coconut and tamarind. Dad's lamb rendang. I steal a piece. So good. He hasn't made it in years.

Dad cut short his work trip to Malawi when he heard about my accident. Since then Mum and Dad haven't left me alone. It's not just because I'm on crutches. They've been feeling major guilt since they found out about Devi and must have made a pact to be more attentive parents.

Just my luck.

I lurch over to the fridge on my crutches and reach into the pocket of my hoodie. There's a little empty rectangle waiting on the fridge. I take Oma's photo out and press it back into place. What would she think of everything that's happened?

My phone buzzes with a message from Rose.

Mel, good news, the magistrate refused Kurt bail on the grounds that he might offend again or interfere with witnesses . . .

Kurt's locked up now, he can't hurt anyone else.

. . . I've passed on your details to Devi. I want to leave it in her hands. I'm sure you understand.

What if Devi never contacts me? Maybe I remind her of everything she wants to forget.

The prosecutors are building their case and five of the eight victims are going to testify against Kurt and the other brothel operators. Devi gave her statement to the police but decided not to stay and testify. She flew home a few days ago.

I lurch to the staircase, pull on the banister and begin the trek upstairs. A dirty black feeling closes in on me. The heaviness in my broken leg spreads to my heart. I fall on to my bed, pull the comforter over my face, and will myself to think nothing, feel nothing.

"Mel, you right?" It's Dad's voice but it's far away, like a doctor's voice when you're coming around from surgery.

Faint yellow light glows through the cross-hatched fibres of the comforter. I don't know how long I've been here. The mattress sags when Dad sits on the side of my bed.

"What's up?"

"I don't know." I hug myself under the comforter.

"You can tell me. I'm not going anywhere."

"Makes a change." I bite my lip and flip back the comforter to grab my phone. "Rose's message," I say, holding it out to him.

Dad's weight shifts when he reaches for my phone. He squints at the message, makes *mm-hmm* noises and works up to a final *I see*.

I pull the comforter back over my head again. "Don't want to come out. Don't want to live in a world like this."

"I feel like that sometimes."

"Why do I feel so bad? Devi's free but what if the traffickers come after her? And Kurt's never going to be punished . . ."

"You don't know that. He probably will. There are five witnesses against him—"

"But not for Devi. Not for what they did to her. No one's ever going to be punished for that." I punch the mattress. "They'll get away with it. And how's she going to live with what they did to her?" The tears roll now. I curl against Dad, my face half-covered by the comforter. He hugs me tight.

"Mel-bee," he says. I unravel when he uses my childhood pet name. "Life can be brutal. Horrible. Unfair." His hand settles on my shoulder. "But in all the crises and disasters I've seen, one thing I've learned is not to doubt people's spirit. Some people have only known cruelty, all their lives. But they keep going. They can be the quickest to find happiness when it visits. It's like pain sharpens their capacity for joy.

"Others break. They live, but it's like holding water in a cracked vessel. No matter how much you fill it, the joy keeps leaking out. But you can't pick which way people will go."

I hope with all my heart that Devi will be one of the strong ones. But the alternative is too sad and my tears tumble again. I turn my swollen eyes away from him.

"Real courage isn't about the big things, the Nobel Prize-winning things. It's the little everyday acts. Getting up when you've lost hope. Trying again. I've seen that sort of courage in many people. Don't underestimate Devi. Look at how she engineered her escape. At least now she has a chance."

He squeezes me hard. "Give yourself time. Stay in bed as long as you need."

FORTY-FIVE

My cast is covered in graffiti. Kind of messy, kind of cool with messages and drawings scrawled all over it. Everyone in our year wanted to put something on it.

Nearly everyone.

The quickest way to the school office is through the admin block. But there's a long stretch of thick carpet in front of me. My crutches keep sticking in it, turning this short walk into a cross-country trek.

Stokes' office is at the end of the hallway. It feels weird to see it again. Ms. Williams, the new counselor, has taken it over. So much happened in there and sometimes I miss talking to him.

Libby appears at the other end of the corridor, looking at her phone, and knocks on Ms. Williams' door. I stop, my skin prickling.

"Give me a minute," Ms. Williams says through the closed door.

"OK." Libby steps back and slouches against the wall opposite. Her head's still down, hanging over her phone.

I could backtrack and go the long way around, but stuff that. My armpits are already aching. And my crutches are so creaky she'll notice anyway. I lurch down the hall – *creak, creak* – struggling with the thick carpet. She doesn't look up. Maybe Ms. Williams might call her in for her session before I reach her.

Did I do the right thing when I finally called the principal? I don't know. But I kept imagining what I'd say to Stokes about it, if we were still meeting up. He made me want to be better.

Libby's on her third strike now and has to see Ms. Williams twice a week. She glances up from her phone for a second and shifts against the wall when she spots me. My armpits are rubbing and I'm starting to sweat. I swing through the last few yards. I'm almost there.

"Cripple," she says out of the corner of her mouth, her eyes back on her phone.

Fuck, I never should have given her a chance. Never should have said all that crap to the Surgeon about Libby needing help not punishment. About wanting her to stop the bullying and sort out her problems. What if Libby has just played us all . . .

She raises her head. Our eyes meet and there's a glint in hers. Not the old bitchy one.

Something different.

Something grateful.

"Psycho," I say.

We both smile.

Ms. Williams opens the door wide to Libby. And I swing past them.

FORTY-SIX

Early spring tumbleweeds of wattle and bottlebrush blossom roll past on my walk home from school. The shop window displays the covers of the daily papers. Every paper has the footy on the front page. With five days until the grand final, Melbourne can talk about nothing else. My nose twitches and I sneeze, but I dig my hands in my pockets and fight the urge to rub my eyes, which are pink-rimmed and bloodshot.

Real attractive.

Since Devi was rescued, the brat camp brochure has disappeared from the fridge. My parents have relaxed – they even admitted they overreacted to The Year I Stuffed Up. I used to think they saw something deeply bad in me, but I've worked it out. They were shit-scared I'd follow in their teen pregnancy footsteps. But that was their mistake, not mine.

This former diehard insomniac sleeps well now, most

of the time. It sounds stupid, but I miss my sleepless nights. It's not the insomnia I miss – that sucked – but the fever that drove me when we were trying to help Devi. Life was intense. Things mattered. I don't want life to become boring. Next month I'm doing a week's work experience with Rose. Maybe playing detective will give me the kicks I need. It still spins me out. Months ago I would have avoided police stations like a cold sore.

School has an easier rhythm now. Libby and I have this unspoken understanding. Sometimes we make eye contact, but we have separate orbits. Maybe she'll deal with her problems, maybe she won't. It's up to her now.

But I still avoid the fort.

There's a fat brown parcel on our doorstep when I reach home. Dad often forgets his watch, glasses, diary, or even his phone on overseas trips and we receive bundles of his lost property from remote locations. I stroll down the path and try to guess where this one's from – Malawi, Sri Lanka, or Bougainville? I go with Sri Lanka.

The parcel's criss-crossed with string and covered in stamps. The brown paper is crumpled and tired, warm from sitting in the sun. I blink hard. It's addressed to me, not Dad. My heart goes a little crazy when I spot the postmark.

It's from Devi.

In the kitchen sunlight streams through the window. I sit down at the table and tear open the parcel. Inside there's a red envelope and a small package wrapped in a batik fabric. The envelope is covered with designs around the border, like those pressed into the diary, but these are hand-drawn in black ink. Devi must have spent hours on the drawings, before she released the envelope and sent it to me.

I slide my finger under the back of the envelope and break the seal. I lay the letter out on the table and flatten the folds. It's written in English. I chew a fingernail and hesitate. All this time I've waited to hear from her and I'd almost given up hope, but now my heart could capsize.

I turn the kettle on. The water rumbles and I eye the letter. It's just paper and ink, but so was the diary. With my eyes shut I wait until the kettle whistles and spews steam. I rub a hole in the condensation on the kitchen window and stare at my reflection. Stop Being A Pussy.

22 September

Dear Miss Melati

I tried writing to you many times. It was hard because you are a stranger and a friend. Now Ibu Yuliana is writing this for me, turning my Indonesian words into English.

After I returned, Ibu Rose sent me Mr. Gerald's letter. He said I was lucky you found my diary because you "would go to extreme lengths to do what's right." It was terrifying putting the diary in his bag. They were always watching.

When I returned everything was different. My family hugged me, but I pushed them away. They told me to keep my secret. But I've done nothing wrong. I really wanted to tell Budi – I tried, but I couldn't. How would he look at me if he knew?

I thought when I came home I'd wake up from the nightmare, but I haven't. There are horrible days when I can see all of their faces. Sometimes I can't sing because my heart hurts too much. But I keep trying because I won't let them steal that too. Next year I will audition for Bandung.

It's only in the last week that I've imagined I could be happy again. I've met an angel – a lawyer called Ibu Mita. She says I have a case against Ibu Sri and she wants to fight for me.

One day I would like to meet you and Michael. I will never forget how hard you worked for me. I pray for you and am sending the biggest thank you, all the way to Melbourne.

Devi

A carving of an Indonesian goddess wearing an intricate headdress falls from the parcel into my lap. My own little piece of Budi. A photo follows. It's Devi in front of her tree, its huge branches ready to embrace her. She holds up a piece of card with TERIMA KASIH MELATI AND MICHAEL written in fat black letters. The afternoon sun touches her – she looks older than I pictured, but there's no trace of what she's been through on her warm features. There's a Budi-shaped shadow in the bottom left corner of the photo. I hold the photo closer and search her darkly pretty eyes for clues to her future.

Michael and I are floating at the end of the lap lane, our feet against the wall. We're here to soak up the spring sunshine. My smile wobbles. I can't get Devi's letter out of my head. Michael was silent for the longest time when I showed it to him yesterday. Like me, he swings between hope and fear for her, but I'm sticking with hope. As Dad says, she's a survivor and at least now she has a chance.

After Devi's letter I feel a bit lighter about Stokes. But among his praise, Stokes had hidden a dig about my dodgy ways, almost like he knew I'd hear his words.

Can't really blame the guy.

Rachel sashays up to our lane in her polka dot swimsuit. Angus trails behind her. They jump into our lane, bombing us.

"Aww, thanks!" I yell.

Rachel laughs and kicks off the wall with Angus, their arms linked, floating past us.

Michael dips his head back in the water and moulds his wet hair into a mohawk.

"Looks good," I say.

"Would you still go out with me if I was a punk?" He does his best sneer.

I cock my head to one side. "Hmm, maybe."

He grabs my ankle, tugging me toward him.

"Not my leg!" My cast is long gone now, but sometimes my leg still feels spongy. Dr. Hoang calls it phantom pain. I panic and kick away from him, crashing into the lane rope. A lap swimmer in the neighboring lane glares at me, does a tumble turn, and speeds away.

"That wasn't funny." When I swipe at Michael's head, he ducks.

"Sorry." His mohawk droops. He dives under and does a handstand. Angus swims up and joins him.

The water is magic. I stretch out, testing my leg. The black line on the pool floor is hypnotic and I zone out and do a lazy swim to halfway down the lane, where Rachel is waiting for me.

"What's that?" She's staring at my hip.

My rash shirt has ridden up and my bikini bottoms have slid down slightly in the water. A chill seeps through me.

"My birthmark."

She bobs closer to me and squints. One dark, wet curl sticks to her forehead.

Here it comes.

"I like it," she says.

"I've always hated it."

"It's better than mine." She pushes apart the hair at the back of her head and displays a red streak, like a graze. "My skid mark. Mum says I came out of the womb too fast."

I laugh and rub my goosepimpled arms. "Mine looks like a pitchfork."

Her eyes narrow. "Nah, it's an anchor. An upside-down one."

"An anchor?" I twist around. She's right. From this angle it does look like an anchor. But when I tilt my head it's a pitchfork again.

Maybe it's both.

ACKNOWLEDGEMENTS

Huge thanks to Linsay Knight, my publisher. From day one you've warmly supported me and been my book's biggest fan. The amazing Walker Books team – Clare Hallifax, Christina Pagliaro, Steve Spargo, Georgie Carroll, and Jarred Noulton – made my debut experience special. Particular thanks to Josh Durham for the wonderful cover.

Thank you to Irma Gold, a phenomenal editor, for your dedication, precision, and encouragement. And to Amelie and Marius for their help with teen language.

A debt of gratitude to Robert Sessions, publishing legend, who backed me and found the perfect home for my book.

I'm honored to have great quotes from the talented and generous Simmone Howell and Lisa Walker.

Jodie Webster read my early drafts without flinching. Your support and insights were critical to shaping this book.

Thanks also to Fleur Ferris, Marisa Pintado, and Luna Soo for your inspired feedback, and to Hardie Grant for shortlisting an earlier draft for the Ampersand Prize.

Terima kasih banyak to Dini Iskurniawati, Olva Ngelo, Petrarca Karetji, Yospeh Yandra, Sukiman, and Inan Ernantriana for making my life in Indonesia so memorable and pretending that my jokes were hilarious.

Heartfelt thanks to all-round rock stars Cameron Macintosh, Rebecca Cook, and Carolyn Court, my earliest beta readers and writing buddies. Your brilliance and friendship (along with a lot of dips and wine) have been the constants through all the ups and downs.

Thanks to the Daggy Dickensians: Katrina Watson, Maggie Baron, Kerry Munnery, Christopher Ringrose, and Peter Kenneally. The Commercial Club writers and the Lazy Writers' Lock-In spurred me on, back when we thought a day was a long time for a lock-in.

I'm grateful to Philippa Martin, Clare Renner, and Antoni Jach for your wisdom, teaching, and encouragement. Thanks also to Antoni for welcoming me into the Masterclass community.

Andrea Cook, Peter and Trish Rankin, and Wendy Caughey gave me quiet places to write, including the Unabomber Hut in Flowerdale (Andrea's description –

not mine). Bridget Williams and David Moore answered my questions about schools.

Rory and Evan Doogan were understanding when I had the study door firmly closed and, along with Eve Williams, generous in providing a teen perspective. Jane Doogan, Pieta Pavan, and Katica Pedisic dreamt bigger dreams for me than I dared to dream for myself.

Leah, Richard, and Paul Bassett inspired my early love of reading and I'll never forget your stunned excitement about my debut. Michael Doogan told me the truth about my first draft without killing our relationship and danced around the house with me when this all became real.

FURTHER HELP AND INFORMATION

For anyone who may be affected by events and issues similar to the themes discussed in this book, the following organizations offer advice and assistance.

If you or anyone you know is in immediate danger, **call 911**.

The **National Center for Missing & Exploited Children** helps find missing children, reduce child sexual exploitation, and prevent child victimization.
Free—24 hours, 7 days
1-800-THE-LOST (call)
www.cybertipline.com

The **National Human Trafficking Hotline** connects victims and survivors of sex and labor trafficking with services and supports to get help and stay safe.
Free—24 hours, 7 days
1-888-373-7888 (call)
233 733 "BeFree" (text)
humantraffickinghotline.org

The **988 Suicide & Crisis Lifeline** is a confidential suicide prevention hotline available to anyone in suicidal crisis or emotional distress. It provides Spanish-speaking counselors, as well as options for deaf and hard of hearing individuals.
Free—24 hours, 7 days
988 (call or text)
988lifeline.org

The **Crisis Text Line** is a nationwide crisis-intervention text-message hotline.
Free—24 hours, 7 days
741–741 "HOME" (text)
crisistextline.org

ABOUT THE AUTHOR

Louise Bassett is an Australian author. *The Hidden Girl* is her debut novel and was shortlisted for the Ampersand Prize. Her award-winning short fiction has been published internationally. After narrowly dodging a career in law, she became an aid worker in Indonesia, Cambodia, Papua New Guinea and Vietnam. Louise now works in community justice. She lives in Melbourne with her partner and too many books.